MURDER
At The Old
EMPRESS

Printed in the United States by
Princeton Academic Press, Inc.
3175 Princeton Pike
Lawrenceville, NJ 08648
609 / 896-2111
First Edition

Publisher's Acknowledgment

ICAN Press would like to acknowledge the following contributors for the production and marketing of this publication: Dahk Knox, Josette Rice, Marian Denson, Steven Fellwock, Patricia Godsoe, Scott Romney and Michael Green.

Cover designed by Steven M. Fellwock

Disclaimer

This document is an original work of the author. It may include reference to information commonly known or freely available to the general public. Any resemblance to other published information is purely coincidental or accidental. The author has in no way attempted to use material not of her own origination. ICAN Press disclaims any association with or responsibility for the ideas, opinions or facts as expressed by the author of this book.

Printed in the United States of America
Library of Congress
Cataloging-in-Publication
ISBN 1-881116-44-1

MURDER
At The Old
EMPRESS

JANNE CAFARA

Published in the United States by
ICAN Press Book Publishers, Inc.
616 Third Avenue
Chula Vista, CA 91910
619 / 425-8945

BOOK ONE

Jade LeMare

The stage is full of human toys
Wound up for three score years
Their springs are hungers, hopes and joys
And jealousies and fears

They move their eyes, their lips, their hands,
They are marvelously dressed
And here my body stands or moves
A plaything like the rest

They play their parts until they fall,
Worn out and thrown away
Why were they ever made at all!
Who sits to watch them play!

-Apologies to Robert Louis Stevenson

CHAPTER ONE

From somewhere behind the earth's proscenium an unseen stagehand was swiftly lowering the curtain of the night. I shivered—not entirely from the cold. After dark, strange cities always have a feeling of unreality. The unfamiliar night scenes gave me the eerie sensation of being in an alien world. And the few cocoon-like shoppers spilling out of the doorways, then quickly disappearing into other doorways, only served to heighten the illusion.

The street lights were anemic beacons as I inched the big station wagon along through the pelting snow. When I lowered the window to get a better view of a twisted street sign, a blast of icy air poured in and almost took my breath away.

The clerk at the hotel had said, "It's only five or six blocks, Miss LeMare. Just go down Parklan to Grand Avenue, then turn left. You can't miss it."

I didn't bother to tell him how easily I could miss it. I get lost in hotel corridors.

The East was having the usual December weather—a howling snow storm, which, according to the headlines, was blanketing the entire Eastern seaboard.

The tinsel-festooned streets were practically deserted but still resolutely gay—like a jewel bedecked courtesan who had dressed for her grand ball and received only a few straggling courtiers.

But, the stage had been set for the Christmas production and, even though it was playing to a half-empty house, the show went doggedly on.

The full-throated loud speakers sang Yuletide carols against the blaring obbligato of the taxi horns. The lifelike toys in the store windows danced their animated stop-time routines.

Pillow-fattened Santas waved their little bells with zealous vigor, prompted, I suspected, not so much by the desire to get something in the pot, as by the fear of freezing to death.

Finally the right intersection. I drove halfway down the block and eased to the curb. As soon as the wipers stopped slip-slapping, large snowflakes began brocading the windshield.

I dropped the keys in my purse, swallowed back the rising qualms and looked across the wide avenue.

The swirling white curtain softened the outlines of the huge old theatre that sat directly across the avenue. Flashing incandescent lights in the upright sign over the marquee spelled out the name, EMPRESS THEATRE.

The glory of the Empress had long since faded, but she was still an imposing old lady. Her ornamental spires and turrets rose haughtily above the seedy pawn shops and dirty store windows filled with sleazy merchandise. Not to mention the darkened doorways that led up to second-story hotels that featured a more saleable brand of merchandise.

Despite a patina of grime, and years of pigeon droppings that dulled her ornate facade—and the word BURLESQUE across the top of the marquee—she sat among her sordid companions grimly clinging to the trappings of her past grandeur.

The candlepower of the colored lights that flickered and danced around the marquee had been dimmed down by a few thousand watts from past years, but they still lit up the name JADE LeMARE quite adequately. And, while it lacked the prestige of the illustrious names once blazoned there, to me,

JADE LeMARE was a most captivating name, even though it was totally fictitious.

My brief span of inflated ego was understandable. In the burlesque end of show business, The Old Empress was the uppermost rung in the ladder. It played only the top names.

For a number of years I'd been a featured attraction, but never in such exalted company. Star billing at the Old Empress was going to be quite a tall feather in my unadorned cap. My agent had assured me that it would open the way to some top flight bookings and higher salaries.

Then why, with all those golden foretokens, did I have such a panicky impulse to escape? To get away from that menacing old ogress who was just waiting to gobble up me and my picayune talents. I felt like a Lilliputian facing the Brobdingnagians.

Finally common sense forced me to recognize my irrational apprehensions. Unfortunately common sense is no match for the mindless fears dredged up by a phobia. In my case, xenophobia. The prospect of opening in a strange theatre with a strange cast and crew always brings on a sense of impending doom.

I touched my medallion of St. Genesius. Over the years, as I groped my way through the labyrinths of show business, he had slain a host of paper dragons for me. Surely he could banish this one. When I looked again, the menacing ogress was just another old theatre, and in a few short days all her strange and frightening children would turn into familiar actors, ordinary musicians and everyday stagehands.

Burying my face in my upturned collar, I went jaywalking across the avenue. Curses from an irate taxi driver fell on deaf ears. I was only concerned in getting inside the theatre before I turned into an iceberg. When Denham said, "An hour's cold will suck out seven years' heat," he must have had this place in mind.

Once inside, I paused to let the warm air thaw out my lungs a little before I started looking around.

In the long ornate lobby, life-sized pictures of the hokey burlesque comics had replaced those of the Jolsons, the Cantors, and the Foys. The famous ladies of Broadway had been displaced by the famous ladies of Burlesque.

The blow-ups of myself on the gold easels were more that just flattering. They were a monument to some retoucher's skill. I walked down the lobby comparing them to their gorgeous competitors. They held their own quite well—I thought. Or maybe I was just whistling dixie.

I went over to the ticket box. "Hi, I'm Jade LeMare," I told the ticket man. "I open Saturday. How do I get backstage?"

"Hello I'm Herbie. The stage door is down the alley to the left of the theatre."

Just then a group of people in full evening dress washed down the lobby and eddied around the ticket box, enveloping us in a cloud of expensive perfume and alcoholic respiration.

The men sported like a flock of top-hatted penguins caught in the grip of a goatish oestrus. They leered at the pictures of the girls and slapped the crook of an elbow as they raised their right forearms in a clinch-fisted gesture of rigid virility.

The women loudly contended they could outpoint the charms of the girls displayed in the pictures—flinging back minks and sables and lifting Paris hemlines to prove their claims.

All members of the better element, of course.

Herbie watched their antics while he collected their tickets. He parried the oblique questions of the men with the adroitness of an old-time politician.

He watched the florid-faced, blubber-bellied member who had lingered behind the others, hastily scribble a note to "one of the strippers" and pass it to him with a twenty dollar bill folded inside. Carefully putting the twenty in his pocket, Herbie tore the note to bits and dropped them into the ticket box.

The pseudo gentleman started to get belligerent, then realizing a fight would certainly entail an explanation to wifey, he followed the rest of the slumming party around the partition, hurling back a string of obscenities toward us.

Noblesse oblige.

"Why did you keep that creep's twenty dollars? I asked.

"He gave it to me, didn't he?" Herbie replied with unassailable logic.

"Time teaches you to put up with ugly things," I quoted. Then said, "Show business teaches you to put up with ugly people."

"And the carneys teach you how to outsmart them." He patted his pocket and said, "Come on, I'll let you out the side door."

I followed him around the partition to the door. He pushed down the panic bar and I stepped out into a windswept alley that ran back the length of the theatre. It felt more like a direct route to the Arctic Circle than an alleyway to a stage door.

I won the battle against the wind for the door that opened into the loading dock. The door to the stage was across on the right. I pushed the buzzer and a chorus girl opened the door, and I was in the biggest green room I'd ever seen.

"I'm Jade LeMare. I open next week."

She waved toward a glassed-in cubbyhole to the right of the door. "Papa Clark will take care of you."

Inside the enclosure a white-haired old man was dozing in a reclining chair, with his feet stretched out to a small heater. I was almost afraid to disturb him. He looked like an ancient mummy that time had forgotten to return to dust.

The top half of the Dutch door was open. I tapped on the glass and a pair of bright blue eyes winked the nap away.

"I'm Jade LeMare. I open Saturday."

"Hi, honey. I'm Papa Clark."

"Who's the stage manager, and where can I find him?"

"Barry Previn. You'll find him across on the other side."

I thanked him, then paused to take in the green room.

The center of the room was dominated by a large round table. Two card tables had cards and games on them. A tired sofa was against the right wall. A niche in the left wall held a coffee urn surrounded by paper cups, dry milk and little packages of sugar and a plate of doughnuts.

A little man in a comic make-up, baggy pants and slap shoes was seated at the big table engrossed in a racing form.

Draped crosswise in a sagging upholstered chair, a chorus girl was half asleep. And at the far end of the room, in the best chair, sat a little spalpeen named Dickie Dougan. Dickie's parents were Tramp and Arlete Dougan—but most actors would swear that Dickie was a by-blow of the devil.

"Why helloooo, Dickieeeee!" I sang out in the asininely bright voice grown-ups use when they're talking to children. "What in the world are you doing here?"

Dickie was blackly silent.

"Oh, come on now," I cajoled. "You're not still mad at me, are you?"

Apparently he was.

Dickie's animosity stemmed from a little incident that had mortified his dignity when I was working with his parents in a theatre in Baltimore.

He was five at the time and typical of the precocious children who are born and brought up in the theatres. He was small for his age, but made up for his lack of stature in pugnacity. He had wise blue eyes that stared out through a mop of unruly red hair, and a face like an Irish cop. Plus the guided instinct for being in the path of anyone running to make a missed entrance.

Before our disagreement my dressing room was his favorite camp. I never accidently shoved him, stepped on his feet, or spilled hot coffee on him. Most everybody else did.

This day he came calling just as I finished putting the final touches on my fabulous new costume. I'd spent a fortune on the material and weeks creating it and sewing on sequins and beads. Today I was going to make a grand entrance in my ravishing masterpiece.

"First act's about over," he said. "You better hurry."

"Yes, I know." I sat down at the make-up shelf and became engrossed in the art of turning a plain jane into a sultry siren.

He walked back to the wardrobe rack. "Is this your new costume?" he inquired.

"Yeah, isn't it beautiful?"

"What's this thing with the beads and sequins?"

"That's a sunburst."

"Looks more like a fried agg."

When I turned around, I discovered he'd been improving on the "fried agg."

He had my tube of glue in one hand and a package of red sequins in the other. He'd squeezed globs of glue on the costume and was sticking wads of the sequins in the gummy mess.

I fought back the urge to kill him.

"You horrible child!" I yelled. "What are you doing?"

"I'm puttin on some more purty sequins for you."

"You've ruined my beautiful costume! You miserable little brat!" I cried. "You're a bad little boy."

"Bullshit, Little Eva," replied Dickie.

He threw the glue and the sequins on the floor, wiped his hands on the costume and headed for the door. But I beat him to it. I grabbed that mass of sheepdog hair, dragged him across my knee, pulled down his pants and spanked his bottom, then shoved him into the hall with his pants around his ankles and his bare bottom in the breeze. For the remainder of my engagement, Dickie and I had been deadly enemies.

Evidently, as far as he was concerned, we still were.

"Where's Tramp and Arlete?" I asked, hoping to thaw the ice. "Are they working here?"

He gave me a look of withering disgust for that stupid question.

"Naw. I'm playin' this date by m'self. I got you down to work in my first scene. You do the old prostitute."

"You know I don't do scenes anymore," I said, as I struck a prima donna pose. "I'm the star."

"You're booked in for the star? Huey oughta sue your agent!"

"Oh yeah? Your mother oughta sue the stork!"

He gave me a Bronx cheer as I went back toward the stage.

I was amazed at the size of the stage. It could've played Sliding Billy Watson's Beef Trust or Power's Elephants.

I went down to the front wings and read the cue sheet that was stuck on the wall under a hooded light.

A balding stagehand with a beer belly hauled himself up out of his chair and came toward me. His progress made a snail look energetic.

"Hi, I'm Jade LeMare. I open Saturday." I was beginning to sound like a parrot with a limited vocabulary. "I was looking to see if I knew anybody on the bill."

"I'm Smitty. Props. Did you find anybody?"

"Yes, Tracy Meade. And I just saw Dickie Dougan in the green room."

He made a sour face. "Oh, you know Dickie?"

"I worked with Tramp and Arlete in Baltimore."

"They're out on stage doing the last scene in the first act."

I moved over behind the proscenium and wigwagged until they saw me. On the Blackout they came rushing off as the band started the fanfare for the current feature. There were the usual effusive greetings. Then we began catching up on what everybody had been doing since we'd last seen each other.

"I've been here so long I go with the lease," said Tracy. "Probably because they can't get anybody else to take the water in the pants."

"We've been here four months," said Tramp. "It's a good place to work."

"They've been giving you a lot of great advance publicity." Darlene said. "You'll have a smash opening."

"She'll prolly open in one and close in the alley!" said a jeering voice behind me.

"Scram, Dickie." Smitty told him. "You know you're not allowed in the wings while the show is on."

Dickie gave him a loud Bronx cheer and headed back toward the green room.

Others gradually joined the group as they gathered for the finale. Tracy introduced three willowy show girls and the comic I'd seen in the green room. Then a pretty blonde woman and Sonny, the house singer.

The comic was Joey Benson. The blonde was Darlene Duvalle.

Joey was a nonentity who had been unhorsed early in the human race. Darlene had a chip on her shoulder and boozy breath.

Smitty shushed the chattering that was getting too loud. Then he jerked his head toward the rear of the stage, "Auh, Christ Almighty!" he grated. "Here comes Old Hot Crotch!"

A spraddle-legged little woman had appeared through the archway from the green room. One of the show girls pushed at her companions and said, "Come on, let's go. I can't stand that silly bitch." They moved away as the woman made a beeline for the group.

She swung her arms briskly as she punched the floor with short mincing steps. What with her high heels and her wide spread crotch, she pranced along like a spavined faggot with jock itch.

Pushing her way into the group, and without waiting for an introduction, she gushed, "Hi, Jade! I'm Lutrica Steiner—everybody just calls me Luttie. I'm the managerial assistant!"

Luttie was instant antipathy. She was obnoxiously self-important and she had that boorish, pushy familiarity which I loathe.

She draped her arm around a chorus boy's shoulder, stood hipshot and began flinging out what she fancied were devastatingly clever quips and bon mots. In the vernacular of show business—she was ON.

It was evident she considered herself a comedienne of the first magnitude. After each one of her gems she'd give a loud snorting cackle.

I nudged Tracy. "I'm surprised she doesn't wear slap shoes and a putty nose."

"I wish she'd wear a muzzle. She's about as funny as an open grave!"

When Luttie wasn't keeping herself in stitches with her own scintillating wit, she was grabbing at the most ordinary remark and trying to turn it into some risque double entendre.

It was difficult to tell which was the more nauseating, her uncouth jokes or her cutsie-pie-isms. Despite her effervescence she seemed to be about as popular as the yaws.

She was never going to win any beauty contests, either. A flat head was connected to her shoulders by a short, thick neck. Behind the Andy Gump chin, another one hung like a frog's pouch. Heavy-lidded eyes completed the amphibian picture.

Small groups of chorus girls began gathering as they waited for the finale. In their heavily beaded costumes, they looked as though they had just danced out of a harem.

There were also eight chorus boys swishing around in their harem pantaloons. They were the only ones that appreciated little Luttie's wit. Every time she spouted off, they'd scream like a flock of kookaburra birds.

After one of her quips she poked my arm and said, "As you can see, Jade, I like to crack jokes!"

Darlene shot her a baleful glare and muttered, "That's not all you like to crack!"

I stared at her, wondering if a brawl would erupt. Nothing happened, so I assumed Luttie hadn't heard Darlene's compliment.

"Outside of being half-swacked, what's wrong with her?" I asked Tracy.

"She hates Luttie's guts."

"I imagine Luttie is rather easy to hate."

"Yeah, her charm starts clotting very quickly."

Just then the feature started taking her bows and everybody ran for their place in the finale.

Luttie's audience had shrunk, but not her repertoire. She told Smitty and me a couple of jokes that would peel the skin off your teeth. The word obscene would have to find a stronger meaning to describe Luttie's brand of humor.

I liked her even less than I liked her humor. Leaving Smitty stuck with her, I moved over into the wings to watch the finale. Behind me, I could hear her voice sawing on and on like a ripsaw through a pine knot. I wondered how much a managerial assistant managed.

CHAPTER TWO

On the blackout, Tracy and Darlene came from behind the curtain feeling their way in the sudden darkness. When Darlene saw Luttie was still there, she curled her lip and grated, "Oh balls! I thought that little cock-walloper would be gone by now!"

Luttie elected to come along when we started across the stage. They ignored her but she wasn't aware of it. She was too busy showering me with her wit.

On the switchboard side I met two of the stagehands. One was John Buick, the flyman. He was short and meaty and insolent. Another was Slim Gerhart, the electrician. He was tall, lean and meticulously dressed. He looked to be in his early seventies. Before I'd finished my first week, I learned that his language usually turned the air blue and the ears of his listeners red.

Then a tall man somewhere near forty appeared at my elbow.

"Hello, Miss LeMare. I heard you were back here. I'm the manager of this place—Huey Ryan. Welcome to the fold."

"Thank you, Mister Ryan. I'm happy to know you."

Huey Ryan was a sorrel-haired man with a pleasant smile and a charming personality. He had a wry sense of humor and a lilt of laughter in his voice. His manner was foreign to most managers—he wasn't condescending to the actors. I liked him immediately.

Tracy tugged at my arm and said, "Jade, this is Chou Chou Morgan."

Chou Chou was a perfect specimen. Tall and handsome with an air of supreme self-confidence and a manner that spelled top banana. He was dressed like a fashion plate, except for a red Windsor tie clipped with an over-sized rhinestone ornament.

"How are you, Miss LeMare?" His eyes focused in on me for a moment. "I'm sure you'll have a pleasant run." He nodded at Tracy. "Let's go over the Billboard scene again."

Tracy looked suicidal. "Again? Again? I could do the thing in my sleep!"

"Well, Darlene can't." His tone implied she couldn't do it wide awake.

As they followed Chou Chou toward the stage, Tracy called back, "Don't leave, Jade. We'll have night lunch after the show."

"You couldn't leave now," Luttie informed me. "You haven't met Barry, yet."

"He's the stage manager, isn't he?"

"You'd better believe it, honey. Come with me, I'll introduce you to him."

Lucky me! Her company had about the same appeal as a three day seminar on sheep dip.

She draped a palsy-walsy hand on my shoulder and ushered me through the archway on the left of the switchboard and out into a long hall.

I was born with an acute aversion to being pawed. I moved my shoulder sharply forward and the cloying little hand fell away.

The hall ran back the depth of the stage. Most of the principals' dressing rooms were along the right wall. Facing the hall at the far end, was a door with the name Barry Previn carved on a wooden plaque. Luttie walked in without knocking.

Barry Previn was a very good looking man. Deep waves of dark chestnut hair crowned a face with hazel eyes, a perfect nose, and a full mouth with a charming lop-sided smile. I guessed him to be in his middle-thirties.

"Barry, this is Jade LeMare, our new feature." Luttie made it sound as if she had just hired me.

"Hello, Jade." He put out his hand. "First time you've been here, isn't it?"

"Yes."

"I'm sure you will enjoy it here. We have a great gang of performers, a good crew—and a mighty fine orchestra."

"Those are some mighty fine pluses."

He was wearing an expertly tailored blue plaid sport jacket with slacks that matched the darker tones. A pale blue shirt and dark blue Nettleton boots tied off the outfit. His clothes were tasteful and expensive and he wore them beautifully.

He had excellent taste in clothes, but it became increasingly clear that he had no taste in women. You needed no crystal ball to discern that Barry Previn had a burning passion for dumpy little Luttie.

He was talking to me about my number, but he couldn't keep his eyes off her. He was watching her with his heart in his eyes and his mind in his pants. Luttie was responding like an alley cat hyped on Spanish fly.

So much for my budding crush.

When she put a cigarette in her mouth and leaned toward him, he took a book of matches from his pocket, gave her a light and handed her the matches.

"Barry always keeps me supplied with matches." She put a hand on his shoulder and gave me a slanty-eyed look—just to let me know who was sitting in the catbird seat.

"Well, you're always out." He made it sound like not having enough brains to carry a book of matches was an adorable trait.

They were scarcely aware of it when I said the usual trite pleasantries and left.

That was copacetic by me!

Going back down the hall, I saw the door at the other end had a lopsided star on it. That would be my dressing room.

There was a sand tub in the area for smoking. Fire laws strictly forbid smoking anywhere else back stage.

To the left of the door an iron stairway went up to a halfway landing, made a U-turn and continued up to a second hallway where the dressing rooms for the lesser principals were located, along with the ladies and gents toilets.

Slim had been explaining the layout to me as I leaned on the guardrail around the switchboard.

"Are you all squared away?" he asked.

"Yes. Barry said he'd have the stage set the way I wanted it done." I added, "He's a very charming man."

"Yes, he's a very pleasant guy," he said with an indifferent shrug. "But he's not too intelligent. And he's a chronic liar."

I had already surmised Barry was never going to steal Old King Solomon's thunder, and I really didn't care if he was running a dead heat with Ananias. I laughed. "Any other qualities?"

"Yeah, everytime he sees a whore, steam comes out his ears."

"That's Barry, for sure," put in John Buick. "He thinks a whore's crotch is the eighth wonder of the world."

The orchestra struck up the overture for the second act and a horde of people came running from everywhere and ran for the stage. I sighed. There was an awful lot of talent here I would have to compete with. But I couldn't afford to get cold feet, now. This was the major league and I'd been waiting too long for my turn at bat.

Had I known the old theatre's sinister secret, would I have been so eager to try for one of the brass rings on her merry-go-round? Would the lure of some future glory have nullified the stalking menace that lurked in the shadowy depths behind the scenes? I think not. Murder is a powerful deterrent.

When I went back to the green room, Dickie was still there. I tried to charm him into being friends again.

It was no go. The conversation was all one-sided.

"Oh, stop pouting," I coaxed. "You know you like me."

"No I don't," he snarled. "You're at the head of my shit list!"

I was searching my brain for an olive branch, when Luttie came prancing in. She immediately launched into her Henny Youngman type comedy. When her audience didn't respond she said, "Well, I've got to get back to killing rats." She flung her head back, crooked a leg up in front and took off pumping her arms a la Jackie's exit.

Before she reached the door, Dickie said, "Good, the ugly on' bitch is gonna kill herself."

"Someday, somebody is going to strangle you." I tried to sound severe, but I couldn't stop laughing.

His pug face split into a grin as he slid out of his chair and came over to stand by me. "Would you want to come to our place and have night lunch with us? I'll tell Tramp and Arlete."

I thought, isn't it strange how a mutual abhorrence can draw people together.

"I can't. I promised Tracy I'd have night lunch with her."

"Where ya gonna go?"

"I think she said Romain's."

"Romain's is a real swell joint and they got good pizza."

As we were leaving the theatre, Tracy said, "Would you mind if Darlene came along?"

"No, not at all."

Romain's exceeded Dickie's plug. It was downright poshy. The low-backed booths were upholstered in red leather and the napkins were real linen. The waiter was taking our orders when a volley of cackles drew everybody's attention toward the entrance. Luttie had come in with Barry Previn and a tallish man, wearing an overcoat that was too long and pants that were too short. He carried his head forward and tilted to one side—

like a one-eyed chicken looking for a worm. He had the pre-
tentious manner of a would-be big shot.

"Who's that one?" I asked.

"That's Bryce Reagan. He's the inner-office coordinator."

"Sounds important. What does it mean?"

"It means flunky," said Darlene.

There was a flurry of waving and yoohooing from their
booth and everybody turned toward the entrance again.

A tall wasp-waisted man with enough black bushy hair to
stuff a mattress had come in and was mincing his way over
to their booth. He was the classic example of a swishing
queen—with the gliding walk, the limp-wristed upturned palm
and the slightly disdainful sniff with the chin above one raised
shoulder. He swept along bowing and apologizing to the diners
if he happened to brush an elbow.

"What does that one do?" I asked. "He's too tall to dance
in the chorus."

"That's Ivan The Terrible. He makes wardrobe for some of
the women." Tracy said. " He's another one of Luttie's devout
disciples."

"Most of the Boys seem to be in her clique."

"Why not?" said Darlene. "She's their little oral surgeon."

"Their what?"

"She's a genius at performing phallic operations."

"Apparently she doesn't charge much for her services. Her
clothes look like she got the last grab out of the grab bag."

"She does a lot of charity work."

"She seems to have quite a stable of admirers."

"Ah, yes," said Tracy. "She's always three-sheeting about
what a femme fatale she is."

"According to her," Darlene said, "she needs a chair and a
whip to keep the entire male population from storming her
crotch!"

The waiter served the food at their booth and there was a
lull as they all started sampling each other's dishes.

Barry gave Luttie a sip of wine, then kissed her.

"Now she'll turn into a beautiful princess," I said.

"The charm backfired on Luttie," said Darlene. "She just keeps turning into an uglier frog."

"He's a very attractive man," I said. "Surely he could do better than that."

"Oh yes, he could do a lot better than that," said Tracy. "In fact, he had a beautiful wife who was a fabulous performer."

"What happened?"

"When she found out he couldn't stay away from barflies and cheap low-class trash, she divorced him."

"How long ago?"

"Four or five years."

"So now, he's free to indulge in his favorite penchant."

"Water always seeks it's own level."

"Tracy," pleaded Darlene. "Will you come in early tomorrow and help me with Chou Chou's lousy scene?"

"Sure. But don't worry. If you foul it up, he won't do anything but throw you into the orchestra pit." When we left, Luttie's snorting cackle followed us out the door.

CHAPTER THREE

In show business, Friday is the end of the week. It is also the prelude to Saturday's phenomenon known as opening day dementia. Before I was fully awake I could feel an onset of the symptoms.

When I opened the curtains to stare out the window, a cold gloomy day stared back. Overhead the sky was a bowl of gray lead.

Except for a trip down to the coffee shop for breakfast, I spent the day in my room, washing my hair, doing my nails and giving myself a gooey mud pack. For the most important opening in my so far uneventful career, I wanted to be pluperfect.

That evening I got to the theatre before the show started.

"Aren't you afraid you'll miss the rehearsal?" jibed Tracy. "You only have about three hours before it starts."

"I wish I had three days," I groaned. "Don't forget this is my first tilt at the BIG windmill."

"Don't be silly. Sho' Biz is Sho' Biz. Little theatre. Big theatre. They're all alike." She stood up. "Let's go meet some of the troupe you missed last night."

The first was Royal Rydeen, the straight man. A decade ago
he'd been a fairly well known Broadway actor. I wondered
what had waxed the skids for his toboggan from Broadway hits
to burlesque bits. My surmise was belles and booze.

Greasepaint and rouge did wonders for his still handsome
face, and a permanent wave did wonders for his thinning hair,
which he wore in a loose pompadour with one careless curl
falling boyishly over his left eye.

His prowess with the ladies was legendary, and obviously
he still considered himself a masterful seducer. His modus
operandi had the stylized perfection of a Kabuki dance. Time
was raising his hairline, lowering his chinline and wrestling a
girdle for his waistline, but he still went through his routine
with each step expertly timed.

He kissed my hand and murmured the kind of silken phrases
that would have charmed a less cynical maiden than myself out
of her scruples before the night was over.

He walked away as though he was taking leave of a goddess.

"Good grief!" I said. "He's got a line that would beach a
whale!"

"Not around here. He tried it out on all of the girls, but they
soon got onto him. When he finds out he can't make a score,
he moves on." She laughed. "He has the same philosophy as
the little dog—if you can't eat it or screw it, piss on it!"

"He must be desperate."

"Oh no, he still manages to snag a barfly off one of the
stools out at the 'body exchange' every night."

Next I met Marc Robling, the chorus producer. He looked
more like a marine sergeant than a ballet master. Piercing blue
eyes took your measure through rimless glasses. He had a
pencil-line moustache and graying hair, that was cut military
style. A ram-rod posture and a brusque way of speaking added
to his martinet manner.

After the formalities were over, he asked, "Have you two
worked together before?"

"Yeah," said Tracy. "We were on a road show together."
"I'll see you later, Jade," he said marching off to his office.
He was a very imposing looking man. He was also a homo.
"I'll bet he is a hard S.O.B. to work for."

"Well the girls know it's their ass to the Indians if they foul-up a routine out on stage. He screams from the wings and threatens to throw the culprit out on her untalented ass before the show is over."

"He sounds like the Simon Legree type homo." I said. "He must have a problem keeping girls."

"No . . . he's never fired one since I've been here . . . and none of them have quit." She seemed puzzled. "I guess they stay because the salary is good—and they have a thick skin."

On the other side I met the powers that be—the two grand moguls who owned the place. They didn't believe in politeness and they did not tip their hats to ladies.

After Tracy performed the introductions, she threw in a few bouquets about my talents as a feature.

Their reactions began somewhere under the heavy padding as they lifted their shoulders in a simultaneous shrug of large disinterest.

Jasper Herlick was a stumpy-legged little tzar with a body that had gone to his belly. His heavy-jowled face was dominated by hooded eyes, a large hooked nose and a rubbery lipped mouth that chewed on a wet cigar, which he shifted constantly. His bullet head sat atop a fat neck that was stiff with its own importance. His partner, Phil Nathan, was repulsive in a different way.

He was tall and skinny with a small head that jerked around on a long stringy neck. Dyed hair was carefully combed across his head to conceal a large bald spot. With a ski nose and a wide mouth, he resembled a none-too-bright ostrich. He carried his expensive cigar between his fingers.

Both were arrogant and over-bearing and—like all little tin gods who wish to be thought important—they talked down to the people who worked for them. Both had been knighted with a diamond pinkie ring.

While they looked me over, Tracy said in a whisper, "The actors call them the Gruesome Twosome."

"You can go out front and catch the show, if you want to." Phil Nathan waved his cigar at the fire door. "Give you a chance to get an idea of our policy."

"Thank you," I said, with what I hoped was the right amount of reverence.

"That's only for this time, though," said Jasper Herlick. "We don't allow the actors to sit in the audience."

I wondered if I should genuflect and kiss his ring.

As I went up the aisle I was hoping they didn't come around too often. Little tin gods expect an awful lot of kowtowing.

I've never been able to sit out front and watch a show. Perhaps because I've seen the same thing a few hundred times from backstage. But this show was something else. It was more like a Broadway musical than a burlesque show. The girls were pretty. The wardrobe was beautiful. The scenery was tops and Simon Legree knew how to stage a show.

"They really put on a first class production here, don't they?" I said to Tracy when I went backstage after the show. "That comedy routine you and Chou Chou did was terrific."

"He's a clever performer, but he's a pain in the bucket to work with." She put on her coat. "Let's go get a sandwich."

In the green room, Luttie and her entourage were sitting around the big table. She and Barry were playing verbal badminton, using dirty one-liners for their shuttlecock. All the Boys were splitting their sides at her humor.

"The comics haven't got a chance against her, have they?"

"If the comics ever used her material the censors would close the theatre."

Half an hour later when we came back, everybody had left the green room except Barry and Luttie.

Barry was seated at the table, ostensibly working on some sort of puzzle. Luttie was draped on his shoulder with her flabby dugs hanging against his ear, supposedly helping him with the puzzle. It was a ludicrous attempt at camouflage.

Her legs were slightly spread and she was grinding her pelvis against his side while she slid up and down, like the widows of some primitive tribes who masturbate on a slanted sapling during a sexual orgy. The table didn't hide the bulge that was threatening Barry's zipper.

On the switchboard side, a small group was watching a show on a television sitting on top of the prop box.

"There's a better show going on over in the green room," Tracy told them. "Better tiptoe though, you might ruin the climax."

"What's going on over there?" Slim asked.

"Old Hot Crotch is jacking herself off on Barry's hipbone," explained Darlene who had just come over from the green room.

"What in the hell does he see in her? She's about as appealing as a dose of the clap."

"You just don't appreciate her repertoire. It's been rumored she has more ways of screwing than a cat has lives."

"Yeah, but what does he do with her after he gets through screwing her?"

Darlene widened her eyes and said, "Why he screws her again!"

"For Christ's sake!" flared Bryce Reagen. "There's nothing between Barry and Luttie but a clean and decent friendship!"

Ivan the Terrible flew into the fray. "Bryce is right!" he stormed. "Just because a man and woman love being together all the time, that's no sign they're having a thing!"

Tracy herded Darlene and me toward the stage. "Let's go out front and watch the rehearsal. Things are getting kinda over-charged back here."

We went out and sat in the third row. Across the aisle, three of The Boys were dishing somebody with relish.

Darlene looked up and made a retching sound, "Ugghh!"

A big dark-haired female had come down the aisle and stopped to talk to The Boys. She flailed the air with large flapping hands as she talked in a breathy Marilyn Monroe voice.

Assuming she was one of the strip women, and, since it is only natural to appraise your competition, I sized her up.

Thick ankles bulged over her shoes. Heavy legs, shaped like stove pipes supported a very large rear end. When she turned to stare at me—the newcomer—I saw a long lantern-jawed face with little simian eyes set under an inch-high forehead. The eyes were all puddled up and the long chin was trembling.

I felt I definitely had this one outpointed.

She went on down the aisle and over to climb the side steps. She canted so far forward from the hips that only her big boxy rear-end kept her on an even keel. She clumped across the stage like a cow on snow shoes and wound up practically on top of Barry.

"Holy Hades!" I said. "They must have hired her in the dark with a sack over her head. What does she use for her billing, The Beast of Burlesque?"

"She's not in the show," said Tracy. "She works up in the office with Luttie. She's the bookkeeper. Her name's Aidey Wojossky. All the guy's call her Twitching Twat."

"I wonder what she's weeping about."

"She's always snivelling about something," Darlene said. "That poor-helpless-little-me act is a pain in the ass."

"Well hers is dist a itty bitty dirl," whined Tracy. "Hers always dot some big ole hateful probby. Her has to run to Barry and let him help her solve them."

"How can he stand to have her slobbering over him?"

"There's nothing like a teary-eyed damsel in distress to bring out the protective male ego," said Darlene. "Makes them feel like Sir Galahad."

Obviously Barry had once again poured oil on the troubled tears. Aidey was giving him playful little pushes and whinnying like a freshly deflowered filly.

"Looks like he has solved her problem again," said Tracy. "He keeps her happy by babying her and telling her what a brilliant genius she is."

She doesn't look too brainy," I said. "But then, nature should have given her something to make up for such a rotten job of assemblage."

Huey Ryan came across stage, stopped and sang sixteen bars of Give My Regards to Broadway, into the mike. When everybody applauded, he lifted his coattails, took a coy bow and skipped down the steps.

"You're a pretty good song and dance man," I said. "You should've been an actor instead of a manager."

"Not me!" he said flatly. "My folks were in show business, it was chicken one day and feathers the next. I prefer a steady diet of steak."

"Gee, Huey," said Tracy. "I didn't know your folks were in show business."

"Yeah, they were a song and dance act. They played all the vaudeville circuits. When I was a kid, they played this old theatre at least once every season. It was my favorite. There were so many places to explore."

Marc strode out onstage and bellowed, "All right, Barry, lets get this turkey on the turnpike."   Huey went up the aisle and we went back to gossiping.

"By the way," I finally asked. "How come you two know all the secrets of Barry's romantic triangle?"

"Promise you'll keep it a secret?"

"Want me to sign a pledge in blood?"

"The sinks are back-to-back on the wall between my dressing room and his office. In order to repair a broken pipe, a plumber had to cut a hole in the wall. He filled the hole up with plaster. One day the chunk of plaster fell out and I could hear Luttie and Barry talking. I couldn't tell what they were talking about until I crawled under the sink and put my ear against the hole."

When I stopped laughing, I said, "Doesn't it get mighty uncomfortable under that sink? Besides, why are you two so interested in a lady killer and his two ugly doxies?"

"Good heavens!" exclaimed Tracy. "Haven't you ever watched a soap opera? Illicit love has a powerful fascination. That's why the old boys in the Bible spent more time writing about those harlots, whores and concubines than they did about virtuous ladies." She lowered her voice and intoned, "And now folks you have just heard another episode in the thrilling saga of Barry Erectus, Hot Crotch and Twitching Twat. Tune in tomorrow for another exciting chapter."

Darlene stood up and wobbled a trifle. "I gotta go get my wardrobe ready for tomorrow." She walked up the steps and across the stage with stiff-legged precision.

"Has she always been a drunk?" I asked.

"No. She was a feature, and a darn good one, too."

"What happened?"

"She was married to a handsome straight man."

"So?"

One morning she woke up and discovered he had cleaned out their savings, taken their new car—and all her jewelry— and left town with a barfly. That's when she started drinking."

"Poor gal," I said. "You only go around once in this life, being married to a whore-loving chiseler can make it a mighty unpleasant journey."

I looked up at the big stage and groaned, "Oh, dear me."

"What's the matter?"

"This place. What if I walk out on that stage tomorrow and die . . . dead?"

"Don't be negative. You gotta think positive."

"Sometimes I wonder if that positive thinking is all it's cracked up to be."

"You're crazy."

"That goes with the profession."

"Don't worry. You still have St. Genesius."

"If you remember, he let the lions eat him."

Marc came down to the footlights and told me I could go over my number while the girls were changing.

I'd been paying close attention to the boys in the pit. Ponti was a leader par excellence. The sax man was crowding Boots Randolph. The trumpet man was another Bix Beiderbecke. But the prize in the crackerjacks was the drummer. Strip women need good drummers like folk singers need guitars.

I climbed the steps, thanking my lucky star for the biggest plus so far.

CHAPTER FOUR

Saturday was sparkling bright and cold enough to emasculate the proverbial brass monkey.

It was dark backstage when I arrived at the theatre and judging by the temperature in the dressing room, the second ice age was setting in. Kicking on the radiator did nothing to stay the encroachment.

The room didn't live up to the star on the door. There was a dressing shelf and a chair. Against the back wall was a day bed that had come down through the ages. A stained sink in the corner, a wardrobe rack and one ancient guest chair completed the sumptuous furnishings.

I performed a passing miracle applying my siren mask, considering my fingers were numb and every time I breathed my magnifying mirror fogged up.

As soon as I finished, I went looking for someone to deal with the heat problem.

Smitty was sitting on Slim's stool behind the guardrail, holding a racing form under the hooded light. He looked up in surprise. "What'ta hell you doing here so early?"

"I always come in early on opening day. I have a million things to do. The first one is to get some heat in that Siberian outpost. Got any suggestions?"

"Old Ned takes care of the heat. You'll probably find him sleeping off a hangover in the basement. He'll be in that little room behind the furnace."

Walking across the huge stage, I could hear my footsteps echoing through cavernous depths of the old theatre with the rhythmic sound of a muffled heartbeat. They seemed to blend with the pulsing echoes from past decades of walking, dancing, shuffling feet. Even when I paused to listen, I could feel the pulsing beat.

A theatre is a living, breathing entity. It's lifeblood is drawn for the legions of actors who have breathed their hopes and dreams, their tears and failures, their triumphs and glory into its heart.

The spirit of every actor comes back to live in every old theatre. The great and the small. The famous and the unknown. They're all there within the walls. They're always there to lend you their immortal armor.

Back when Dickie was five, I used to take him into my room and tell him stories. One night I told him a story about the spirits of actors who come back to live behind the footlights.

He shook his head. "No they can't. Arlete says when you die, if you're good, you go to heaven."

"That's for all other people. The actor's only heaven is behind the footlights."

"I'm glad we've got one of our own. I wouldn't never want to be nowhere I couldn't be backstage—and play show."

Like everything else in the old theatre, the basement was immense. To the far side was a door with a sign, MUSICIAN'S ROOM.

I knocked on the door behind the furnace and an ancient man opened the door and his eyes at about the same time.

"Hi, are you Ned?"

"That's what they call me." He yawned widely.

"I came down to see if you'd turn on the heat."

"Oh lordy, looks like I done overslept again." He polished his glasses and began fiddling with some knobs. "It'll come on right quick, now."

I thanked him and started back, then paused as I passed a hall to the right of the stairs. At the farther end I could see a carved wooden horse from an old carrousel. Being fascinated with old relics, I went back to take a closer look and saw there were other old props and cast-off pieces of scenery. There was an old H and M wardrobe trunk—locked tight. I poked at a few things then went back to the main part of the basement.

Old Ned was standing between the hall and the bottom of the steps. He eyed me with a sharp probing look.

"Ain't no use you noseying around down here looking for it," he said. "You won't be finding nothing down here."

Did I only imagine the hostility in his voice?

"Looking for what?"

"For whatever 'tis you're looking for." The suspicion that showed in his eyes wasn't my imagination.

"I wasn't looking for anything," I protested. "I only went back there to look at that old merry-go-round horse."

It was plain he didn't believe me.

Smitty was still handicapping the morning line. "Did you have any luck?

"Well yes . . . but Ned didn't seem to think I was down there to see about the heat. He acted like he thought I was down there hunting for something."

"Don't pay any attention to Old Ned, he's about two foot out of plumb." Smitty went back to his racing form.

I went back to my dressing room and tried to relax. Out in the hall I could hear the signs of the awakening madhouse.

Opening day in any theatre is always the equivalent of a "Hey Rube" call. High-keyed temperaments held in check by sheer force of will, are likely to erupt into volcanic violence at the slightest provocation.

One actor rushes wildly after another, to go over, once again, some bit of business or some scrap of dialogue.

Anxious chorus girls are going over their routines.

Amateurs, coming down with a severe case of stage fright, walk around like staring zombies or laugh shrilly at nothing. Stage managers with clipboards hurry after principals and stage hands. Chorus producers just have raging hydrophobia.

And over-riding the bedlam on stage is the cacophony of musical instruments being tuned and tootled in the basement. But somehow, when the curtain finally rises the melee quietens like a lullabied baby.

Someone tapped on my door. I opened it and stepped out in the hall when I saw it was Marc.

"Well, the show can go on now. Miss Delilah Laine has just arrived!" He put his hand on his hip and camped like a prima donna. "She didn't show up for rehearsal last night because it was simply too cold. Can you imagine that?" He lifted his eyes heavenward, "Well, to hell with her! She's so damned skinny, every time she does a grind and bump, her pelvic bone rattle. Wait 'til you see her!"

At that moment, as if to be accommodating, the lady appeared.

I understood why he had been communicating with heaven. She had the face of an orchidaceous angel and a red crowning glory that cascaded to her waistline. She was wrapped in a divine mantle that must have depleted half the nation's mink population. Her fingers dripped with a multitude of celestial rubies and emeralds—and a few old dirty lousy diamonds.

I just stared.

She didn't.

She swept passed us as though we were painted on the scenery. Pushing open a door of a dressing room half-way down the hall, she aimed a command at Marc.

"Will you get this pigsty cleaned up?"

Marc, who could upstage with the best of them, said he wasn't the janitor. If the place didn't suit her—she could damn well clean it up herself!

That's when I learned the lady had some non-heavenly attributes. She fired off a barrage of profanity that would have felled a roustabout. When she ran down, she went inside and slammed the door.

"Temperamental bitch!" Marc went down the hall to his mauve lighted atelier and slammed his door.

I went back inside and closed the door. It was getting near curtain time and the last-minute frenzy was gaining momentum.

I heard Tramp unlocking their door and Arlete telling Dickie to behave himself and stay out of everybody's way. As soon as they closed the door, Dickie went calling on the new co-feature.

Miss Laine made it clear that she did not care for small-type visitors. She threw him out.

In a moment I heard her heels come clicking down the hall and out onto the stage. Doubtlessly on her way to the basement for a talkover with the musicians. After a while she returned and went clicking back down to her room. Instantly, there was a bellow of rage and the crashing sounds of a loud scramble.

I opened my door in time to see Dickie come streaking down the hall, followed by a bottle of My Sin that shattered against my door-jamb a hairbreadth from his head. A torrent of profane threats followed both of them.

"Stay out of here, you little pug-faced bastard! If you ever come in here again, I'll kick your goddamned ass, you little son of a bitch!" Miss Laine stood in her doorway holding a pair of blue pumps in her hand. She kept on swearing with hail-stone velocity.

The commotion flushed Marc. He came charging out of his office demanding to know what in the hell was the matter with that temperamental bitch now? His towering fit of rage threatened to outstrip her own.

"That little bastard pissed in my shoes!" she yelled. "I caught the little son-of-a-bitch doing it!"

Miss Laine's penchant for the finer points of the King's English wasn't the only thing about her that left me in pop-eyed amazement. The fluttering wisp of chiffon she was wearing for a robe was like a barbed wire fence—it protected the property but it didn't obstruct the view.

The view was an eye popper. It exposed the largest pair of love muffins I'd ever seen. Plus the fact that the rest of her was so thin you could count her ribs. It gave the illusion of a pair of gourds hanging on a slatted fence.

The argument kept going from bad to worse. There were dire threats of cancelled contracts, law suits, and a kick in the ass if she didn't shut her filthy mouth!

She tried to shut his by throwing a sloshing shoe in his face. Which elevated the screamfest to monumental heights.

Huey arrived and used tact instead of Marc's brand of persuasion. With masterful diplomacy, overlaid with flattery, he finally got her calmed down.

Dickie was hiding behind my wardrobe trunk.

In the lull after the storm, a beautiful blonde girl made the turn in the stairs and paused on the landing. She put her hand to her mouth and called down soft voice, "Is it safe?"

Marc looked up and smiled. "Yes, it's safe, Caralyn." He smiled sweetly. "We've got her caged."

Last night when I heard her singing at general rehearsal, I had been deeply intrigued by Caralyn Ayres.

The natural quality of her voice showed years of expensive training. Her speech and manners had been polished in some gilt-edged finishing school. She was obviously from a world as far removed from burlesque as the crab nebula. With her talent she had the open sesame to any door in show business. With that beautiful face, she could launch a thousand career ships— so what was she doing in a burlesque show?

Barry Previn tapped on my door, "Stand by, Jade. You're almost on."

A troop of butterflies started fluttering their sand paper wings under my breast bone and the enigma of Caralyn Ayres faded into a blackout.

Barry was waiting when I opened the door. "I just wanted to tell you I'll be singing your trailer. Sonny is in a snit because he got his notice, so he developed a sore throat. What do you use for your build-up?"

"Nothing at all. Just tell them who I am and don't use more than three adjectives."

"Good luck, Jade."

Out on stage I arranged myself on the red velvet chaise lounge and tried to find a juju to vanquish the butterflies.

Then in swift sequence, Slim pulled the blackout, the band picked up the fanfare, and a small shadow darted from the wings and scared me out of my few remaining wits.

Dickie clutched at my arm as his words rushed out with desperate haste. "Jade . . .'member them dead actors you told me about . . .the ones that come back to help you not be scared? Well you don't havta be scared . . . ever'damn one of them is in the wings!" He barely outraced Bryce Reagan off the stage.

Then I heard Barry use up the three adjectives, wait for a four bar intro and start singing.

I took a deep breath and relaxed as I felt the real world receding swiftly away.

The curtains parted slowly and the special lavender spotlight wrapped me in its glowing embrace. The butterflies were no longer imprisoned under my breast bone, they were silver-winged fairies dancing in the lavender light. The stage stretched like a magic carpet—waiting to take me to that magic world of make-believe where myth and fantasy become reality.

The music wove itself into a sensuous melody and the blue velvet backdrop caressed by dancing shadow.

The audience sat silent and waiting, their upturned faces eddying like a field of daisies in the twilight. Would their silence turn into a serenade?

At the end, I removed the net brassiere and stood poised in the magenta spot while the waves of applause swelled and billowed around me. Then on winged feet, I twirled toward the proscenium and posed on tiptoe, waiting for the waves to subside.

In a daze of triumph I heard Barry say, "You were sensational, my lass. Right down to the last bangle."

I came back to reality and began pulling tissues from a box taped to the back of the tormentor, to mop the ice water from my palms and face.

Belatedly I managed to gasp out a breathless, "Thanks, Barry. You were wonderful. You sounded exactly like Bing Crosby."

"You're welcome. I was trying to sound exactly like Bing Crosby."

Waiting for the girls to finish the finale routine, I felt myself winding down like a spent top. Then there was the bow in the finale. The curtains closed and my wardrobe girl was waiting in the wings with my robe.

It was over. I had survived another opening in another strange theatre.

BOOK TWO

Anthony Clay Blake

The best laid schemes o' mice and men
ofttimes gang agley.

Robert Burns

CHAPTER FIVE

"Mister Gardner wants to see you, Mister Blake." Although Miss Pryn's words fell with their usual business-like precision, there was an "I know something you don't know" in their tones. However, her cool impersonality forestalled any questions. Miss Pryn was a sleek, chic greyhound of sophistication with wide blue eyes and a charming smile, but she did not waste them on the lesser members of the firm.

I said "Thank you" to the back of her head and wondered why Mister Gardner wanted to see me. It didn't take too long to find out.

Without preamble, he informed me that the firm was merging with a larger corporation and would retain only select personnel from each firm. Along with my salary, there would be two week's severance pay waiting for me at the cashier's cage. He hoped I'd have a nice Christmas and a very prosperous New Year. And it had been a pleasure to have me with the firm.

And that was that.

And I was Anthony Clay Blake, bright young scientist out of work.

The news was a rather jarring surprise. Even though there had been an undercurrent around the office lately. I had assumed it was due to pre-holiday lift. It wasn't too surprising that I'd heard none of the rumors. I'm not strong on inner-office sociability, therefore I don't make friends among my co-workers.

I was beginning to resent getting fired. Not that it really mattered. Although it had put a slight stopgap in my plans. For a long time I'd planned on two things—making a name for myself in science and marrying Lela Mellon. Any setback was annoying.

I finished emptying my desk, picked up my checks and went down the hall toward the elevators.

On the way home, I had dinner in my favorite restaurant, then stopped in the Fireside Club for a drink. The place had a four-piece combo that played good music. I had sung there a few times before. Before I'd finished my drink, the leader came over and said, "How about a couple of songs?"

"Sure, why not."

I went up on the bandstand and sang a couple of numbers from the Hit Parade. A man at the end of the bar kept nodding his approval in tempo. When I sat back down, he came over to join me.

"Pretty fair set of pipes you got there."

"Thank you."

"Where are you singing?"

I looked at him blankly.

"Aren't you a singer? Professional, I mean."

"No."

"You should be, you sing damn good."

"Thank you," I said again in what I hoped was a polite dismissal. He smiled amiably and left. I wasn't too surprised to find he'd merely gone to get his drink.

His hair was graying at the temples and his nose showed the skill of a plastic surgeon. A dead cigar was clamped between his teeth. He talked around it with amazing facility.

"Ever think of going into show business?" he asked.

"No."

"You should. You got a mighty good voice and you got a lot of know-how." He nodded approvingly. "You got the looks too. They're all big pluses." He took a card from the watch pocket of his Brooks Brothers suit and handed it to me. "If you ever decide you'd like to try the business, drop around and see me."

"Thank you, but I'm not interested in show business." I said goodnight and left him sipping his scotch.

At home, there was a letter under the mail shute. I recognized my mother's handwriting. I read the letter twice before I could believe what I was reading.

The gist of it was, my father hadn't left us as well off as I'd always thought. Somehow all the money was gone. My mother had taken a mortgage on our home. Two payments were overdue. Could I send enough money to cover them immediately?"

I was dumbfounded. What could she have done with all the money? The stocks? The bonds?

I endorsed the two checks and put them in with a letter telling her not to worry, I'd be up as soon as I could and take care of everything for her.

By the next weekend I discovered I had seven dollars and thirty cents. Never before in my life had I been without money. I began going through the pockets of everything hanging in the two closets, to see if perchance there might be a dollar or two.

I found a gold pen in my brown suit. There was also a stick of chewing gum and a business card. At first the name Dave Stern meant nothing. Then I remembered the night at the Fireside.

As I started to drop his card in the waste basket, the memory of his offer to place me as a singer floated through my unfocused thoughts like a bobbing straw. I turned the card in my fingers and let the memory slowly crystallize into an idea.

I had spent the last ten days being interviewed and leaving resumes at various firms and hadn't received one call back.

Evidently there was a plethora of junior grade scientists leaving resumes. I began to speculate what it would be like to be a professional singer.

The map showed Dave Stern's office was located on a street I'd never heard of.

On the streetcar, I felt a growing sense of excitement. I hummed a melody of one of the latest tunes and made a mental note to buy some song sheets.

Two blocks from the streetcar stop, I found the address and surrendered myself to the vertical thrashing machine. Inside, with my arms and legs intact, I glanced around for a directory.

The elevators were spewing streams of odd-looking people out into the lobby. Seconds later, they vacuumed in an equally odd looking stream.

The men wore their overcoats pushed back under their arms with their fists jammed into the pockets of their jackets. Most of the girls looked as though they had just recently escaped from an impoverished Gypsy camp.

Mister Stern's waiting room was a cubbyhole furnished with a plastic couch and a matching chair. Behind a half partition to the right, a red haired girl was busily typing.

"I'd like to see Mister Stern."

She spoke into an intercom and motioned me toward a door marked PRIVATE.

Mister Stern was massaging away the traces of his nap. He smothered a yawn and said, "What can I do for you, young man?"

"You offered me a job as a singer."

"I did?" he said blankly. "When?"

I reminded him about the night he'd seen me at the Fireside.

"Oh yeah. Yeah, sure. Now I remember you." He waved toward a chair. "Have a seat . . . sit down."

He got his cigar going with one hand while he shuffled through the debris on his desk with the other. He found a book and began leafing through the pages.

"Let's see . . . they need a singer over at the Empress."

I hope it's a nice club—like the Fireside."

"It's not a club. It's a theatre."

"A theatre. . . ?"

"Yeah, a burlesque theatre."

"Burlesque! I wouldn't go inside one of those dives!"

He shrugged, raised his eyebrows and pulled down the corners of his mouth, simultaneously.

"Forgive me," he said piously. "I'd forgotten your exalted character."

"And I misjudged your's."

"Well, I wouldn't want to corrupt a member of the better element. So . . . good day, young fellow."

I had reached the door when he said, "The salary is two hundred a week—plus half a day for the midnight show." He rolled his cigar to the other side of his mouth and blew smoke at the ceiling. "You could learn a lot. A hell of a lot of top stars today learned their trade in burlesque."

I hesitated, but I couldn't backtrack. You can't lower the standards of a lifetime for a few paltry dollars.

"I still wouldn't consider working in one of those places."

"Suit yourself."

When I hesitated still longer, he scribbled an address on a slip of paper and held it out to me. A knowing smile quirked his mouth when he said, "If you change your mind, you can go over and audition. I'll call Marc and tell him about you."

"I won't change my mind." I declared. But I went back and took the slip of paper.

When I got back to my apartment, I had four dollars and I hadn't had lunch. Reluctantly I put my watch, a pair of cufflinks and the gold pen on the table. That was the extent of my pawnable assets.

I wasn't sure of the procedure of pawning one's belongings. And I had no idea how much to expect.

The balding little man at the pawnshop poked at the things with an uninspired forefinger. He put a glass to his eye and examined the watch. "Fi'teen dollahs fa th' lot."

"Fifteen dollars? I expected a lot more."

He shrugged. "Nobody's gon' give you moah."

I took the fifteen dollars.

A hamburger took the place of lunch and I started on another round of futile interviews with personnel managers. By five o'clock I was exhausted.

The hamburger had decimated the fifteen dollars and bus fares had whittled it down still further. Dinner in a cheap restaurant left me with five dollars.

I spent the evening listening to Mantovani and trying to think of a solution. One fact kept coming to the top—you can't live without money!

After a practically sleepless night, that fact had registered very clearly.

The idea of working in a burlesque theatre was abhorrent, but with a five dollar bankroll I had no alternative. Two hundred a week was more than I'd been getting—junior scientists don't command large salaries.

I spent more time than usual selecting what to wear. Thank heaven, I still had a selection. During the long ride I stared out the window and hoped the singing job hadn't been filled.

CHAPTER SIX

The Empress has seen better days as a once top vaudeville theatre and, despite the run down look and the garish banners, it still had an air of imposing opulence.

It was impossible not to stare at the life-sized pictures of the half-nude girls that lined the lobby.

"I'd like to see the manager," I told the man at the ticket box.

He jabbed his chin at the mezzanine stairs and said, "Up the stairs. Office is the first door on the right."

The plate on the door said, MANAGER. I opened the door and walked in. Behind a big desk in the corner, a smartly dressed man was talking on a phone. The nameplate on the desk said, HUEY RYAN. He smiled and nodded toward a chair.

The office was a large room with ceiling-high windows overlooking the marquee. The furnishings appeared to be the original ones. They were solid and expensive, but they had seen a lot of service. Their air of Victorian propriety contrasted oddly with the frame photographs of scantily-clad girls in seductive poses that covered the walls. They were all inscribed, "To Huey" with varying messages of endearment.

I was vaguely disappointed to find Huey Ryan a likeable, intelligent-looking man with a nice smile. I had prepared myself for something between a hoodlum and a procuring moron, and I didn't like to be proven wrong. He hung-up and looked inquiringly.

"I'm Anthony Blake. Dave Stern sent me over to audition for the singing job."

"Oh, then you want to see Marc Robling, the chorus producer. You'll find him backstage. Go back out front and down the alley on the left side of the theatre. You'll see the stage door. He smiled pleasantly. "I'll catch you tonight at rehearsal."

As I stood up to leave, two females came out of an inner office and he introduced them to me. Luttie Steiner and Aidey Wojosky. Even the most charitable of critics would have instantly classified both of them as dogs.

Aidey Wojosky was a big awkward creature with a baboon face. Frustrated sexual desire had made a mess of her complexion. She had legs shaped like a goalie's shin guard, and big box-like hips. Her simpering giggle sounded like a coy loon.

Luttie Steiner was a little woman with a thick neck and a pair of receding chins. Bulbous, washed out blue eyes were vacant except for the raw lechery in them. She was as subtle as a prowling alley cat, as she looked me over with bold inviting glances. Clearly she considered herself an irresistible sexpot. She flirted and posed seductively and laughed like a braying donkey. She was totally insufferable.

"I'm the managerial assistant," she informed me.

I didn't wait to find out what a managerial assistant was. Giving Huey Ryan a quick nod, I said goodby to the Mutt and Jeff barracudas and made an impolite escape.

The alley led to a door big enough to run a boxcar through. Beside it was a small door with a sign, STAGE DOOR NO ADMITTANCE. It slammed against my heels as I stepped through into a large area, obviously used for loading and unloading scenery. The only other door was across the area to the right. I pushed the buzzer and waited. There was a metallic thud and the door was opened by an ancient pink-cheeked man.

"I want to see Marc Robling."

"All right, son, come on in." He indicated a large archway to the left. "Just go out there on the stage— somebody will tell you how to find Marc."

I went through the archway and onto the stage, then stood there feeling conspicuous and ill at ease.

Two uniformed policemen who had come inside to get a respite from the frigid weather were drinking steaming cups of coffee while they watched the girls. A pretty girl in a fifth avenue suit was teasing them about their avid interest in the girls.

Four girls were standing in the wings under a bank of colored lights. Short strands of beads shimmered around their hips and thimble-sized cones were glued on their breasts. Outside that, they were nude.

Lying on a platform was a startlingly life-like mannequin. It was small and beautifully molded, and completely nude except for an infinitesimal chastity belt. It had the exotic features of an Eurasian princess. Even the long black wig looked real.

The music changed tempo and the mannequin sprang to life yelling "LOOK OUT! I'm on. I"M ON!" She snatched up two large folded Chinese fans and dashed for the stage. Trying to open the fans at full gallop, she tripped on a coil of cable and sprawled flat on her belly at my feet. I helped her up, made some brushing motions in the air around her and asked if she was hurt.

She shook her head angrily. "No. But I missed my entrance and Marc'll pitch a hissy."

One of the girls dancing near the wings grabbed the curtain and pulled it a little ways out on stage. When it swung back, it revealed the mannequin in a September Morn pose . . . then she went into a dance routine. The blue light made the blotches of dirt from the floor stand out starkly on her white skin.

I looked around for someone to ask about Marc Robling. It felt like I'd been standing there for hours. I'd never been back stage before, but even to my unpracticed eye this place looked like the honky-tonk level of show business.

I buttoned my overcoat and went back toward the archway. The pretty girl deserted the officers and headed me off.

"I heard you tell Papa Clark you wanted to see Marc."

"Yes, but I haven't found him." I said shortly.

"C'mon, I'll show you."

Following her as she led the way through the jungle of junk at the rear of the stage, I made an effort not to brush against the stacks of top-heavy scenery. I didn't want to get filthy, or brained.

"Watch out for the cables." She eased past a throne chair on a dias and rounded a corner. "You can get across back here behind the backdrop." She waved her hand at the murky gloom like Moses commanding the Red Sea to part. "Just tell Slim you want to see Marc." Before I could ask about Slim, she was gone.

Halfway over, there was a pair of sliding metal doors in the back wall. The room beyond was filled with racks of brightly colored costumes.

The other side of the stage was dominated by a long wooded rail with wooden pins through the top bar. Sets of rope came down from somewhere above and were looped around the pins. The front wall was taken up by a large switchboard with an iron guard rail around it.

There was a man sitting behind the guardrail. I walked over and said, "Are you Slim?"

"That's me."

"I'm looking for Marc Robling."

"I'll take you to his office in a minute, soon as this number is over." He looked me over and said, "Are you the new singer?"

"I don't know. They haven't heard me sing yet."

"You can't be any worse than Sonny." He nodded toward a wispy young man who was singing into the microphones. "As far as he knows, pitch is something you do with horse shoes and baseballs."

Two iron stools took up the space between end of the switch-board and an archway out into a hall. Across the hall steps went up to a landing that turned and went somewhere above.

A small boy was sitting on the bottom step, playing with a magnet. He'd put it on the floor and inched it along until it clanged against the iron riser. From under a mop of red hair, he was looking me over like a horse-trader rejecting a club-footed nag.

Slim pulled the blackout switch, waited a second, then flooded the stage with bright lights.

"Okay," he said. "Come on."

When we went down the hall, I noticed the small appraiser got up and trailed along. Slim knocked on a door painted red.

"Someone to see you, Marc."

A fiftyish man with a sheaf of music in his hand opened the door. He was ramrod straight and had the bearing of a Prussian general. The most piercing blue eyes I'd ever seen regarded me through rimless glasses.

"He's your new singer." Slim called over his shoulder.

"Good. I was just getting out the music for next week. Come inside and I'll explain it to you. He pushed the door all the way open and I had a full view of the room.

It was a hell of a bailiwick for a Prussian general!

The walls were painted rose, the ceiling was midnight blue with silver stars pasted thickly in it. A sagging sofa with the legs sawed off, was covered with a black embroidered shawl, with long red fringe. The shelf was draped with a length of purple velvet and the lights were shaded in mauve silk scarfs. The odor of Woodhue washed over the scene.

"What's your name?" He asked absently.

"Anthony Blake."

"I'm glad to know you, Tony. Just call me Marc."

He handed me some slips of paper with song lyrics on them.

"Are these for the audition?" I asked.

"Audition?" he hesitated. "What theatre did you work at last?"

"I've never worked in a theatre."

He stared at me as though he hadn't heard me right.

The little brat on the sofa scoffed, "Geez Chris', he ain't nothin' but a dum' amachure, Marc. You might jes' as well keep Sonny."

Marc said, "Shut up, Dickie! But apparently he was considering the suggestion.

Sonny went by the door singing Mister Paganini and that threw the decision my way.

"Well, I can't stand that caterwauling any longer. We'll find some songs you know and I'll tell the comics not to put you in any scenes."

"Can you acksully sing?" asked the imp on the sofa. "Or are you one them guys that gets up in a barroom and makes a jackass outta hisself?"

"I assure you I can sing." I said sharply.

"Good", said Marc. "Go out and find Caralyn and see how you two sound together. We'll rehearse after the show."

I went back down the hall with mixed feelings. Just beyond the archway to the stage a group of people were standing around a tub filled with sand, smoking and talking. I paused, intending to ask one of them how to find a girl named Caralyn.

There was a click of heels on the iron stairway. I glanced up and felt my face flush, but I was powerless to lower my gaze. My heart skipped a beat . . . then started drumming a tattoo under my ribs. I stood there angrily willing myself not to respond to the thrill that was sending hot tingling sensations through my veins.

I wondered if the people around the sand tub had noticed my staring. It wouldn't have mattered—since I seemed to be unable to take my eyes from the vision on the stairs.

Coming down the stairs was the most beautiful pair of legs I'd ever seen. My eyes followed them upward as they flowed into a body of exquisite perfection. She was wearing a sheath of gold material that molded itself to every curve of her body.

As she gracefully descended the steps, the slit in the side of the costume revealed a glimpse of white skin from her knee to her thigh. The clinging gold material outlined the smoothly rounded hips and the full firm breasts.

Her face had the elusive beauty of a Renoir painting. The shaded light above the stairs made coppery highlights in a cloud of topaz-colored hair.

She paused on the bottom step to regard my gaping, then stepped down onto the floor in front of me. I caught the scent of her perfume and began having trouble with my breathing.

She looked up at me without lifting her head. I wondered if it was a seductive trick or a natural mannerism. Whatever, the effect was magnetic. The large jade-green eyes had the lure of the ages buried in their depths. It was like looking into deep pools of sea water and losing yourself in the weaving green shadows.

Slim said, "Tony, this is Jade LeMare, our feature. Jade, this is Tony Blake. He's going to be the new singer."

"Hello, Tony." Her voice had the soft blurring of the South in its tone.

"How do you do, Miss LeMare." I knew I sounded stiff and coldly formal, but I had a sharp feeling of resentment toward her. I resented the uncontrollable emotions she aroused in me.

"Looks like I'm doing very well—don't you think?" There was no mistaking the mockery, it sounded as though she'd been reading my thoughts.

She turned toward a door with a star on it. I knew the exaggerated sway of the hips was for my benefit. As she turned to close the door, there was a smirk of amusement in her smile.

I turned my back and went out onto the stage.

CHAPTER SEVEN

Luttie was perched on one of the stools at the end of the switchboard telling dirty jokes to a sandy-haired man who was leaning on the guardrail.

"Bryce, this is Tony Blake, our new singer. Tony, this is Bryce Reagan, our inner-office coordinator."

Bryce was one of those people who affect an air of detached superiority in hopes it will fool somebody into thinking he's important. He acknowledged the introduction with a slight nod. Evidently amateur singers were not too high in his pecking order.

Luttie propelled herself off the stool and grabbed my hand. "Come on, I'll let you meet our stage manager." She towed me back to the far end of the hall, and walked in without knocking.

An attractive, smartly dressed man was standing at a drawing board blocking out something on a sketching pad.

"Barry, this is Tony. Marc just hired him to take Sonny's place." She pawed at my arm. "Tony, this is Barry."

"Glad to know you, Tony." We shook hands. "Tonight is general rehearsal. You open on tomorrow's matinee."

"Tomorrow?" I stumbled over the word.

"Don't worry about it. Marc and I will change a couple of numbers and ease you in gradually."

"Thank you. . ."

"Luttie, why don't you take Tony out and let him meet some of the people? Then take him out and let him see the show."

Each introduction was seeded with her idiotic efforts to be the clever comedienne.

The pretty girl was Tracy Meade, the talking woman. Didn't all women talk? Then there was Darlene Duvalle, her eyes were too bright and her tongue a bit thick. A tall shapely woman with waist-length red hair, a haughty air, and the friendliness of a tong ax man was Delilah Laine the co-feature.

Dickie had trailed along like a bad penny.

When I uncoiled Luttie's fondling grip and told her I didn't want to see the show, she whirled off and left me standing.

"Why'nt you wanna see the show?" asked Dickie. "It's a real good show."

"I'm afraid I couldn't sit still that long."

I didn't want to see the show because I didn't want to sit among a crowd of depraved morons howling their frenzied appreciation of off-colored jokes and cheap half-nude women. I knew I wanted no part of this sleazy business or its low class people. All I wanted was to find the quickest way to the exit.

"Wanna cup of coffee? There's some in the green room."

"I'd rather go outside for a while."

"Sure," he said. "It ain't nuthin' to be ashamed of. All amachurs get it."

"Get what?"

"Stage fright."

"I thought you got stage fright when you went on stage."

"You do. But it starts buildin' up on general rehearsal. Time ya go onstage tomorrow, you'll have rigga mordis."

Wise little brat!

"The joint at the alley's got good samitchs." He looked at his over-sized wrist watch. "Rehearsal starts at midnight . . . better be back 'fore that, though."

No need to tell him that I wasn't coming back.

After paying the fat woman behind the counter, I had less than four dollars left. If I went without breakfast, I still wouldn't have enough to go job hunting tomorrow.

I had no choice. I went back down the alley to the theatre. The show was over and a lot of people were wandering around trying to find out about things from somebody else. Most of the things seemed to be still up in the air.

Marc steered me to a short flight of steps. "You'd better sit out front until we need you—you'll get killed in the stampede up here."

He raced back to the center and began barking commands and making explosive gestures, until he got everybody in the exact formations he wanted. Then he came hurtling down the steps and sat in the front row to view the results.

Halfway through their maneuvers, he catapulted out of his seat and charged the steps like Teddy going up San Juan Hill.

"Will you unpack your brains out of the moth-balls and try to remember what the hell you're supposed to be doing?"

He herded them back into their original formation, leaped over the footlights and ran backwards up the aisle, screaming profane directions at the top of his lungs.

Alas, the troops must have been wearing ear-plugs. They made the same mistakes—plus some extra ones.

He raced back up the steps, raised his eyes heavenward with a sigh of pained resignation. With elaborate courtesy he explained it all over again. Then he struck a graceful pose, draped his hand on his hip and glided along in a pointy-toed walk. He was dripping politeness when he explained, "You're supposed to walk like houris—not whoreys." He took out his handkerchief, tore two strips and tied them around the ankles of the worst offenders and purred, "There. Now maybe you can tell your left from your right."

He came down to the footlights and said, "All right Ponti, let's try it with the music."

The orchestra played the intro and like the stroke of a magic wand the white lights went out, turning the stage into a moonlit south sea island. Hidden fans gently swayed the palm trees. The colored lights created the illusion of a dreamy island paradise. Beautiful girls in sarongs began dancing to the strains of "The Moon of Manakouri."

When the number was over, Tracy came on stage wearing an over-sized queenly gown, which she held out from her body with a gesture of acute distaste.

"Marc, I'm not going to wear this facocta thing!" She unfastened the gown and let it fall down around her feet, then kicked it toward the wings.

"The number won't be anything without that little touch of comedy."

"I think it would be better done straight."

"Well I don't," he shouted. "It's supposed to be funny."

She gave a flirt of her toe toward the facocta thing and looked as if she were going to throw up. "Well, this thing certainly won't make it funny."

"Then goddammit, don't wear it!"

"I wasn't going to."

Marc suddenly changed tact. He paid her some lavish compliments and ended by saying he liked to use her in his numbers because she had so much sparkle and talent and absolutely no one had her flair for comedy . . . etc . . . etc.

She pushed a palm toward him to stop the flow. "All right. All right. Don't drown me," she pleaded.

"Then you'll do it like I want it?"

She gave him a smile of mock delight and carolled, "How could I refuse after all that smaltz?" She held it at arm's length. "It smells worse than it looks."

She carried it off stage as though she had a bundle of last year's garbage. At the front wing, she stepped aside to let a girl I hadn't seen before come past her.

The newcomer had been cast in a different mold than that of her co-workers. She looked more like a mainline debutante than a member of a burlesque show. She was beautiful and marvelously put together, and her air of ultra-elegance was not a pose. She had ingested it along with her pabulum.

"Where's the new singer?" she asked Marc.

Her manner of speaking could only have been cultivated in some very expensive finishing school.

"This way, dear." He held out his hand to help her down the steps and I noticed a vast difference from his usual manner. He was actually gracious.

"Carolyn Ayres, this is Tony Blake. I have you two down for a medley in the opening."

"What are the songs?" I asked.

"Broadway Rhythm. Broadway Melody. Lullaby of Broadway."

Thank heaven, they were all oldies and I knew the lyrics.

Marc leaned over the orchestra rail and told Ponti we were ready to go over the opening medley.

On stage I asked Carolyn, "What do you sing? Lead or harmony?"

"It doesn't matter. I can do both."

As we finished, the quiet was shattered by a burst of applause from the wings. For an instant, the outside world seemed remote and unreal. Here in the darkened theatre was another world, secret and hidden, a magic place where magic people lived. It was an exhilarating sensation.

"You were sensational," said Carolyn. "I was surprised to hear you sing pop. I thought you'd be more on the classical side."

"It doesn't matter. I can do both."

"Touche!"

Jade had dragged Slim's stool out to the front wing. She had her heels hooked on a rung and her chin in her hand.

It was irritating to find her there.

"I didn't know I was going to have a jury," I said coldly.

"Of course not. We didn't want you to get the blue funks."

"Well, what's the verdict?"

"You'll do." She stood up, pushed the stool back in place and left.

The stage was overflowing with principals, chorus girls and boys. Many of the women had been surreptitiously eyeing me as they moved around. I pointedly ignored any of their attempts to start a conversation.

That night, lying in bed, I told myself I'd stay at the theatre until I found something in my own field. I cursed the ill-fated luck forcing me to accept a job in a bawdy burlesque show. Being on a stage before a crowd of moronic perverts would be humiliating and degrading. But I would have to do it for awhile. Because I'd been forced to realize you can't live without money.

CHAPTER EIGHT

I was standing before the big mirror in the hall, critically inspecting my image in its first full dress suit. I set the top hat at a more jaunty angle and decided I looked quite dashing and debonair.

Last night, Marc had asked if I had a full dress suit. I admitted I didn't.

He explained where I could rent one and said the theatre would pay for the rental.

"Not a bad lookin' monkey suit." Dickie's laugh sounded like a derisive bullfrog. "Makes you look like one, too." He was occupying the only chair in the hall as though by sovereign right. He waited for my reaction to his barb.

I pretended I didn't know he was there.

Chou Chou stopped beside me and stared at my face. "Don't you have any make-up?" he asked.

"No."

"Then you'd better borrow some."

"Why?"

"Because without make-up you'll look like a corpse."

"That's better than looking like one of the chorus boys."

"Okay," He shrugged. "But under the lights you'll look like you're dead."

"Jeez Chris', Chou, let 'im look dead! It's his funeral."

Jade came through the archway from the stage. "Good morning, Tony." She inspected me and the suit. "My, my. You certainly do look elegant."

"He looks like the undertaker done a bum job."

"Dickie isn't very diplomatic," she smiled down at him. "But you do need to put on some made-up."

"I don't have any make-up," I said shortly. "I wouldn't know how to put it on if I did."

She unlocked her door, hung a very expensive mink coat on a hanger and motioned me inside. "Come on in. I'll give you your first lesson in the art."

"Thank you, but I prefer not to wear all that goo."

She examined me for a moment, then made a prissy face and tilted her chin up in the air. "Is everybody from New England as sticky as you are?"

"What makes you thing I'm from New England?"

"That accent sure didn't come from Texas."

"You're right. I do come from there. My father's people have lived in New England since before the Civil War."

"Do tell."

Those little words with that tinge of derisive amusement in them irked me. "I'm very proud of my ancestors!" I snapped.

"Ah so," she made a slight bow and singsonged, "Reverence for on'rable Chinese ancestors only exceeded by reverence for on'rable New Engrand ancestors."

"The Blakes are one of the oldest families in New England."

Another bow. "Ah so, Jukes fam'ry was old fam'ry, too."

She pushed me toward her chair and stood facing me. "I don't care whether you wear any make-up or not," she said in her sultry voice. "But if you don't, from the front your face will look like one big blank blob of dough."

When I didn't answer, she said, "Dickie go borrow Royal's make-up box."

Dickie banged on a door down the hall and bellowed, "Royal, can I have your make-up box? Jade's gonna put it on the amachure."

She tucked a towel under my collar and began smearing the greasy stuff on my face. "This is Rugged Suntan— guaranteed to make every lady in the audience swoon."

"Do you have ladies in the audience?" I asked snidely.

"I don't know. We don't ask for their ancestral lineage."

When she leaned over me, I could smell the fragrance of her hair and body. Her closeness stirred my senses and the feel of her fingers touching my face started those tom-toms beating in my chest. Once again, I was aware of the ambivalent emotions she aroused in me. It made me angry—angry because I couldn't stop myself from wanting her. I had always harbored a strong distaste for women of her kind—and I still did. But I couldn't turn off my desire for her.

When she picked up her lipstick brush I grabbed her hand. "Absolutely no lipstick!" I said. She shrugged and put it down.

"Your mouth is exactly the same color as your face. The audience doesn't have sharp enough eyes to discern the difference. Unless you accentuate your lips, you will not have a mouth—just a big black hole in your face—with teeth." She explained it all in a patient monotone as though she were teaching Dickie his kindergarten lesson.

I allowed her to use the brush.

She removed the towel and handed me the top hat. "There, now you look a little better."

I looked a lot better, but I wasn't going to tell her so.

Carolyn stopped in the door. "The opening is almost on, Tony. We've only got a few minutes." She led the way behind the curtain out onto the stage. "Don't be nervous. If you foul up, I'll carry you."

"I'm not nervous at all," I said. "Why should I be?"

Then I heard the orchestra playing the intro to Broadway Rhythm—and suddenly I was in a nightmare. Hordes of demons were clutching my throat. A giant boa constrictor was squeezing all the breath from my chest and horned dragons were gnawing their way out of my stomach. The velvet curtains were writhing monsters. The stage stretched like an endless desert. With each step the center mike receded like the waters in Tantalus' lake.

The audience sat silent and waiting, their upturned faces eddying like sun flowers in hell. Would their silence turn into derisive laughter?

From somewhere in the nightmare, I heard Carolyn begin singing. Only when she took my hand and gave it a shake, did I come in with the harmony. My voice sounded hollow and quavery.

After an eternity it was over and I was in the wings and Carolyn was handing me tissues to wipe the cold sweat from my face.

When my breath slowed down to normal, I turned to move out of the wings and saw Dickie at the end of the switchboard. "Well," I said. "Were you satisfied with the amateur's performance?"

"Nah. I wuz wishing you'd forget ever' dam word and then fall in the orchestra pit."

Impudent brat!

Back in my dressing room, I began taking deep breaths, trying to relax.

Someone tapped on my door and I felt a surge of annoyance. Why did these people keep offering their helping hands?

"Come in."

Jade came in with a cold soda. "The ministering angel bringeth relief for thy hot dry stone of a tongue and thy parched desert of a throat." She held the bottle toward me.

My impulse was to refuse it. I didn't want any favors from

her. Accepting favors leaves you obligated. She seemed puzzled as she came a step nearer and put the bottle in my hand.

I sucked the icy liquid into my bone dry mouth and felt the coolness in my throat. I took another long swallow and said "Thank you."

"You're welcome." She smiled at me and those green eyes seemed bottomless. The flawless artistry of her stage make-up gave her the enticing sensuality of Circe. My silence made her ill at ease.

"I'll go . . . so you can change your wardrobe."

"Why should I change my wardrobe?"

"You wouldn't want the audience to think you didn't have a change, would you?"

"Frankly, I haven't."

"Didn't you bring your tux?"

"No."

"You should have it for your spot." She frowned. "Oh well, the matinee isn't too important, but you'll have to bring it for tonight. Saturday is the BIG night. All the better element come slumming in their tuxedos and minks and poisonous manners. For them, one must be sartorially correct."

Should I tell her that the only tuxedo I owned was an outdated model being devoured by the moths in my mother's upstairs hall closet?

Not likely.

"And be sure to have your tonsils tuned. The Gruesome Twosome will be out there tonight."

"The Gruesome Twosome?"

"They are the charming gentlemen who own the place."

"Thank you again," I said. "You've been a great help." I sat back down. "I don't know what I'd have done without you." I didn't try to disguise the sarcasm. And I put a lot of dismissal into the words.

Her face went remote and still.

You're welcome . . . in spades. It's always a pleasure to be helpful." She lifted her hand. "Good luck."

Unaccountably I felt a twinge of remorse. Couldn't I have shown my rejection of her tentative overtures without being so blatantly rude?

Barry Previn came in to tell me to standby for my number.

"Would you like me to give you a few pointers?"

"No, thank you," I said. "I can't remember anything right now."

"I know how you feel, but maybe I'd better show you where to enter and exit."

"Thank you." More helping hands.

"You won't have to sing Jade's trailer. She just now asked me if I would do it."

I was thankful for that. I didn't know what a trailer was.

We passed the little groups that always gathered between the smoking area, the doorway, or the switchboard. While waiting for my cue, I could hear snatches of their conversations. Most of their jargon was totally incomprehensible. They talked in half sentences, broken words and lots of hand gestures. Slim used profanity and obscenities as though they were an integral part of the language.

I was sure I had recovered enough poise and confidence to do my specialty with ease. I was sure—until I heard Barry giving me a star-studded introduction. I entered through the center of the curtains and held onto the center mike. In a foggy-minded trance, I got through the songs without forgetting the lyrics. I was astounded when I received a solid round of applause.

Slim nodded, smiling approval. "You did all right!"

"Only next time don't run into the proscenium. It's hard as hell on the teeth," said Dickie.

The jury had been in the wings again. They came crowding around to congratulate me.

Barry put out his hand. "You were great. I caught you from out front."

It struck me as being rather silly to shake hands with someone over a performance, but I couldn't very well refuse.

Luttie bobbed her head from the group by the pinrail. For once her mouth wasn't going, but her silent message didn't need words. She put out an elongated tongue, slowly sucked it back into her mouth through pursed lips, then winked and wiggled the tip suggestively between the lips.

What a crude tramp she was!

Jade came out of her dressing room in a beaded costume that revealed more than it concealed.

"Hi, sex goddess," said Royal Rydeen.

"Hi, yourself."

She stopped to speak to Barry, then went to take her place on the stage. No congratulations from her. She didn't even glance my way.

I was amazed when Barry Previn started singing. He had an excellent baritone voice and he knew how to use it. He could've given me a lot of pointers.

"He could've been a professional singer," I said to Slim.

"He was, for years."

"With his looks and talent, he should be at the top."

"My boy, talent is the least part of success in sho' biz. To get to the top you have to have a driving ambition and a lot of phenomenal luck." He smiled wryly. "That's about ten percent of what it takes."

"What do you have to have for the other ninety percent?"

"Brass balls!"

"Then I'll never get to the top—not that I would ever want to. I have no ambition to be in show business. This is only a temporary job."

"Then you'd better take a lot of preventive medicine while you're here," he cautioned. Show business is as contagious as the plague. Once you've been bitten by the bug, you've got it for life. There's no known cure."

"Don't worry. I don't need any precautionary medicine. I'm not that susceptible."

"I noticed that. I saw Old Hot Crotch sending up smoke signals for you."

Of course I knew who he meant. "She's embarrassing. "She's too over-eager."

"Yeah, little Luttie is eager as hell." He spit between his teeth. "She's always bucking for a fucking. Gang banging the faggots is her specialty."

"Does she have anything to do with producing the show?"

"Hell no! Her only connection with show business is when she's stretched out screwing some musician or stagehand. Right now, she's got Barry Previn pussy-whipped to his knees, so he lets her throw her weight around back here."

The orchestra picked up the finale music and Barry came running for the side mike. As he announced each name they came from opposite sides and took a bow. He put his hand over the mike and called, "Come take a bow, Tony."

He announced my name and I walked out into the spotlight. I felt a thrill of pleasure when I heard the solid applause.

Then everybody, except for me, backed up as Slim pulled the blackout and John Buick closed the curtains.

Too late I backed and tried to find the center opening. After an eon of flailing wildly at the curtains, I bolted for the front wings.

"Hurray," said Dickie. "Fer a mimit, I thought you wuz gonna stay out there and do an olio act."

I didn't know what an olio act was, but I wasn't going to ask the small Socrates. I started for my dressing room, but sat down on one of the iron stools when I found my legs had suddenly turned to rubber.

The girls were coming off stage, chattering and laughing. Delilah Laine came off in a temperamental seizure.

"This is the first goddamned cemetery I ever saw where the dead sit up and look at you!" She snatched her robe from the girl who was holding it for her and stalked into the hall, leaving an odor of My Sin and a stream of profanity floating behind her.

Caralyn, Tracy, and Barry stopped in front of me. "The

reaction is almost as bad as the stage fright, isn't it," said Caralyn.

"Yes," I admitted ruefully. "I think it might be worse."

"If you don't feel like doing the numbers in the second act, I'll do them for you," offered Barry. "Caralyn and I sound pretty good together."

I was sorely tempted but I said, "Thanks, I'll be okay. I may as well get used to it."

Barry went across the stage and we three went out into the hall. Some of the girls had stopped at the sand tub for a cigarette. Luttie was there and, of course, she had the overriding voice. She was bragging about her college degrees.

Tracy made a sad moue. "She could've had another degree, but she had to drop her major subject."

"Why?"

"She had signed up to major in penology—she thought it was the study of penises."

"That'll teach you not to play straights for Tracy," said Caralyn.

"Thanks. I'll know better next time." I went to my room.

Royal Rydeen knocked and entered. After congratulating me on a fine performance, he got around to the real purpose of his visit, which was to acquaint me with the things that men of his type think all other men want to know.

"If you'd like a drink, there's a bat cave next door run by a long-fingered thief named Curley."

"I don't do much drinking."

He admired himself in the mirror and smiled at my reflection. "And in case you get horny—you don't have to go short. Just drop your pants and Luttie'll be on it like a duck on a junebug."

"That thought is too repulsive to consider!"

"Don't get hoity-toity." At the door he said, "No hard feelings, I hope." And laughed at his pun.

The second act was an anticlimax. When it was over, I hurried to my room and collapsed in the old chair that smelled of dust, mildew and sweat. The actors called it flop sweat.

After a while I felt myself begin to relax and my hands stop shaking. I smiled at the man in the mirror and congratulated him. He had survived his opening performance in show business. If singing in a burlesque house could be called show business.

BOOK THREE

Jade LeMare

For of all sad words of tongue or pen,
The saddest are these; "It might have been."
John Greenleaf Whittier

But sadder by far is to come to your end,
And know in your heart; It could have been.
Irish

CHAPTER NINE

Ever since that first day, when I stood on the landing and looked down the stairs at the handsomest man I'd ever seen, I had been intrigued with Anthony Blake. I smiled as I came down the stairs. But when Marc introduced us, Mister Blake's greeting was cold and formal. Despite that, I was very much aware of his masculine magnetism. I have a weakness for handsome men with dark eyes and black curly hair.

Then after his trauma of facing an audience for the first time—when I had played the role of the Good Samaritan and been given a cold shoulder for my gracious performance—I reluctantly had to concede that Anthony Blake had some glaring flaws in his character.

His rebuff had smarted. I was only trying to be kind to the amateur within the stage door. So, I decided to avoid him for a while, until he'd had time to digest his butterflies and become accustomed to the alien planet and its inhabitants.

As it turned out, stage fright and strange surroundings had nothing to do with his attitude. But due to a woeful lack of perception, I wasn't to find this out for some time.

It took only a couple of days for my smarting to subside and I went back to being kind to the amateur within the theatre.

When he still remained impervious to my timid attempts to give him a bite of the apple—while keeping the serpent out of sight—I knew I'd have to find other tricks for getting better acquainted. And that required more ingenuity than I possessed. How do you let a man like Mister Anthony Clay Blake know you're attracted to him, without letting him know you're in cahoots with the snake?

I'm shy and backward. Backward as opposed to forward—not backward as opposed to bright. At first, I'd felt merely letting him know I was alive could hardly be misinterpreted as forward.

Therefore, my new format had me sitting on one of the stools at the end of the switchboard, in my prettiest robe. That way, while pretending to be mingling with my peers, I was in a position to return a smile in case he should happen to bestow one on his way to the coffee urn.

Then gradually I realized that posing seductively on an iron stool wasn't getting me anything but a cold bottom. Sauntering past his door, on the way to visit Tracy, wasn't working out too well, either. After two weeks he still acted like I'd strangled his grandmother.

A certain amount of reserved aloofness has been held as a surefire method of attraction. But I, and most of the other ladies of the ensemble, discovered that Tony Blake wasn't playing the game of "hard to get." He was simply a snob with a high opinion of himself and a low opinion of actors. He was in Rome, but he damn well wasn't going to discourse with the Romans!

Which, I suppose, from his viewpoint was understandable.

Small-time actors are a cliche-ridden tribe. Any question or statement is invariably answered with an appropo cliche or a hackneyed wheeze from a blackout, or the latest catchphrase from a current television show.

Actors, stagehands and musicians don't have the time, the inclination, or the brains to indulge in scholarly discourses. The actor is busy changing wardrobe, watching for his cues, and preening himself before the mirror. The stagehand is busy shifting scenery, watching for his cues, discussing the baseball scores or handicapping the racing form. The only thing they know about Socrates or Plato or the Philosophical Pleiad, is whether a horse by that name is running in the first at Hialeah. Consequently, most conversations are carried on in passing and all of them are banal and superficial.

Under those circumstances, who could blame Mister Anthony Clay Blake, of the New England Blakes, if he spent his spare moments talking to Caralyn Ayres instead of us ignorant clods.

He casted not his pearls before actors and stagehands lest they would have trampled them under their cliches.

Anthony Blake and Caralyn Ayres had been spawned in the rarified realms of society. Theirs was a natural gestalt. They gravitated together like two shipwrecked literati who had been cast adrift on a sea of ignorance. All their conversations were sprinkled with anecdotes from their respective realms. They usually sounded as though each of them had a copy of the Upanishad tucked under an arm.

Like my peers, my speech was saturated with the patois and idioms of show business. But I was doubly cursed. There were a lot of old saws and maxims left over from my backwoods origins. All that, plus my ingrained shyness, didn't exactly make me a scintillating jawsmith. Needless to say, I was ill equipped to join in their conversaziones.

Neither of them ever voluntarily joined in any of the small groups yakking around the sand tub. If one of them got caught between the switchboard and the wings, while waiting for a cue, they listened politely to the babble, but they only took part if a remark was directed to them.

Caralyn was a quiet, very pleasant girl and everybody liked her. When she was caught in the trap, the men laundered their language considerably. Most of them minded their language in front of the women, but with Caralyn it was more drastic—they practically became gentlemen.

Ah, but with Anthony Blake, that was a pony of another paint job. When he was caught in the trap, profanity punctuated with obscenity was apparently the only language they knew how to speak. They needed a string of four letters to make even the simplest sentence understandable. They had him labeled as a high-toned snob with an exalted opinion of himself. They took a fiendish delight in outraging his aesthetic gentility.

Delilah Laine and Darlene Duvalle, along with Slim, did nothing to contradict his opinion that all show people were misbegotten vulgarians and we ecdysiasts were the worst of the lot.

My daydreams always ran afoul of these insuperable barriers. Still I went on building my fairytale romance, because my sense-data told me that I had a king-sized crush on Tony Blake.

This morning I had paused by the switchboard to give fate another chance, then decided to go to my dressing room and face the disheartening truth. There was only one more week left on my contract. Even Jezebel couldn't bring off a seduction in that short time. On the other hand, maybe Jezzy had never been as desperate as I was.

This week he was singing, "That Old Black Magic," for my first trailer. Sometimes when he stood in the darkened wings and watched me as he sang those provocative words, I fancied I was disturbing his high-toned libido quite a bit.

Lord knows, I tried!

Each time I came within his range of vision, I used every sensuous wiggle and tantalizing gesture in my repertoire. I even stole a few from some of the more bawdy ladies I'd seen.

But, so far, he'd always left his whetted libido behind in the wings.

Ah well, who knows what tomorrow, and Kismet, might bring?

Dickie came sidling through the door. After stalling a while, he leaned against my chair and put his hand on my shoulder.

"Jade. . ." He caressed my shoulder with affectionate little pats.

"Yes. . ." I mimicked his dulcet tones and waited. When Dickie got clubby, the clubee usually got the wrong end of the stick.

"Are we real good friends—like we used to be?"

"Of course we are. Why?"

He closed his fist over my small pearl-handled knife. He saw me watching his reflection in the mirror and gave me a smile filled with pure guile. This was his latest attempt to wheedle me out of the knife.

"I'm still not going to give you my knife. I use it on my cuticles."

"You don't hafta give it to me—I'll buy it."

"Ha. I don't want any of your old lead stage money."

"I found some new stage money. It looks like real gold."

"No sale."

"Aw, gee, wait'll you see how pretty it is." He took his hand out of his pocket. "Shut your eyes and hold out your hand." I did, and he put something in my palm. "Okay. You can look."

I opened my eyes and almost gasped when I stared down at a Saint Gaudens twenty dollar gold piece.

"There, I bet you ain't never seen no stage money that purty. . ."

"Nope. I never did. Where did you get it?"

"I found it."

"Where?"

"Round the theatre somewhere, I don't 'member."

"Dickie!"

"Well, I don't!"

"Well, whoever lost this is probably looking for it."

"Nobody looks for prop money when they lose it. They jus' go in the prop room and get some more."

"This one is different. Somebody may have had it for a good luck charm. You'll have to ask everybody."

"No!" he stormed. "No matter if nobody lost it or not, somebody'll say they did!"

Dickie didn't know how right he was.

"Does Tramp and Arlete know you found it?"

"No. Les' us jus' keep this for our own secret." He shoved the knife in his pocket and made a hasty exit before I could protest that I didn't want to trade.

The coin was dated fifty years earlier. Someone could have lost it years ago. I locked it in my trunk. If no one asked about it before I left, I'd give it to Arlete to keep for Dickie.

Just then, Tracy came rushing in. "Jade, go in my room and man the listening post!"

"Why?"

"Darlene and I have to do the Crazy House scene," she said. "Old Hot Crotch just went into Barry's office with the girl from the box office—they're good friends."

"Who cares about them and their gossip?"

"Hurry up! We might miss an important chapter!"

I felt like nine kinds of a fool crouched under a sink with my ear to a hole under a pipe. The first thing I heard was the girl asking, "What's happening?"

"It's that damned sniveling bitch, Aidey!" raged Luttie. "She knows Barry's crazy about me, but she's so fucking neurotic, she thinks she's still got a chance. I ought to have Huey fire her ass out of here!"

"Well, you know helpless little Aidey has to have Barry help her with her problems."

"What problems?" grated Luttie. She just uses her problems as an excuse to run back here, so she can paw all over Barry while she comes in her drawers!"

"Calm down, you've got nothing to worry about. She's harmless."

"I know that . . . but today she started hinting about having a very big secret. . ."

I stuck the plug back in the hole and went back to my room.

Tracy and Darlene were pretending to be tearing out their fingernails. "Well!" they demanded in unison.

I repeated the conversation and said, "Much Ado About Nothing." Just two rutting dogs snapping at each other over a stud."

"I wonder what Aidey's big secret could be?" said Darlene.

"Maybe hers got herself preggy. Hers always saying she wants five little kids."

"If she ever has five kids, she'll have to find five blind men who are mighty hard up for a screw," said Darlene. "She couldn't get herself a mercy screw at a bachelor convention."

"Let's close this episode," I said. "It's pretty boring."

Out on the stage there was a lot of excited whispering going on among The Boys. I guessed Luttie had filled them in on Aidey's latest ploy.

For some strange reason, The Boys loathed Aidey as fervently as they adored Luttie. They usually referred to her as that big ugly weirdo. Or, That big cock-hungry klutz. Or, that pus-faced creep. All the titles were aptly descriptive, especially the last one.

Aidey's concupiscent juices were constantly oozing out of the pores of her face. As they dried up, they left a little glob. Her hands were usually busy picking off the little globs.

Tony Blake came from behind the backdrop and the canine ladies and their snarling faded into a blackout.

I arranged myself on one of the stools and tried to look nonchalantly voluptuous.

Alas, my act fell flat.

He didn't even glance my way.

Once again, Lady Luck had done an Off-To-Buffalo and left me marking time.

CHAPTER TEN

Next morning I awoke earlier than usual, stretched sinuously and wondered why I felt such joie de vivre. I swung my feet to the floor, feeling the urge to be up and away.

Opening the curtains, I watched the snowflakes piling up on the window sill. On the rooftop of the building across the street, miniature white cyclones would spring up, do a madcap dance among the chimneys, then whirl themselves away over the edge.

On the sidewalks far below, snowcapped umbrellas had created a race of giant toadstools, racing along banging their pilei together.

I looked up into the falling flakes and smiled at a childhood memory—Mother Carey was picking her goose.

Turning back into the room, I began picking up clothes I had shed on the chair last night. They gave off a faint odor of stale cigar smoke. Cigar smoke? Ah, then I remembered. Now I knew why the morning was so blithesome.

Last night, after the show, the Gruesome Twosome came into my dressing room. While puffing on their smelly cigars, they informed me that it would make them very happy if I would extend my engagement for another four weeks.

I said yes, trying not to show how happy it made me.

It meant cancelling a tentative date in Florida, but I would have cancelled a concrete date in Paradise for another four weeks at the Empress. Neither Florida nor Paradise had Anthony Blake as an inducement.

Three cheers for my lucky star! The Gruesome Twosome had given me a second chance to snare the prey.

After a moment, the bubble began to deflate. Although I'd been given a second chance, I hadn't been given any new lures to bait the trap.

I'd already used up all my best tricks. Such as wiggling my derriere enticingly at him on stage. And smiling with snaky charm every time I could arrange to encounter him. These wiles had proved remarkably ineffective.

Until now I'd never had to stalk the prey. My few flings of romantic dalliance had come about solely as the result of mutual attraction. Tarzan love Jane. Jane love Tarzan. Climb tree together.

Milton said, "Yet have they many baits and guileful spells to inveigle and invite the unwary." Too bad he didn't tell us what they were. I certainly could use some of them.

On the way to the theatre I was too cold to plan baits and guileful spells. Walking in a winter wonderland may be a joyful event for poets, song writers, and polar bears—but not for me. By the time I reached the theatre, I was turning blue.

For once Old Ned had the furnace going full blast.

When I finished gilding the lily, I put on a frilly robe and opened the door to let in a breath of fresh air.

Actually the room wasn't all that stifling. I was hoping Tony would be in the hall. Dan Cupid and I needed an early start.

Tony wasn't in the hall, but Luttie was. She was going through exaggerated motions of tiptoeing in and out of dressing rooms. When she got to mine she was full of secrecy and over-blown silliness.

"I'm giving Barry a surprise party," she said. "After the show everybody will wait in the green room until I bring Barry in—I'll keep him busy in his office while everybody is getting dressed." She raised her eyebrows half way up her Neanderthal forehead and smirked significantly.

She handed me a large birthday card. "When you sign it, write something real cute."

I opened the card and read the various greetings. Aidey had written, To Barry, with all my love forever. Your Aidey.

"You will come, won't you," urged Luttie.

I started to refuse. I'm not a party goer. But on the merest chance that Tony might be there, I accepted. Then I gave in to a wicked urge to needle her.

"Looks like Aidey is mad about Barry. Aren't you a bit .jealous?"

"Who'd be jealous of her?" She snatched the card out of my hand and was gone.

As she left, Tracy came through the door. "Were you invited to the claim staking?"

"Claim staking?"

"What else? You heard her raving about Aidey running back here to paw all over Barry. Well, this party is her way of letting Aidey know she has first claim on the property."

"What about Aidey? What if she doesn't take the warning?"

"That weeping willow! She's no match for Luttie. She'll back off like a scared rabbit."

"Speaking of the lady!"

Aidey had come through the archway and stopped by the sand tub for a few puffs. She was obviously dressed for the party. She was wearing what looked like a gray flowered feed sack with a gathered flounce from knees to the floor. Draped around her shoulders was a crocheted shawl with stringy fringe.

Her makeup looked as though it had been applied by the Braille system. She threw the cigarette in the tub, dabbed at her eyes with a tissue and went down the hall to Barry's office.

What a pukey klutz she was!

"Looks like hers has got another old problem," said Tracy.

"Who cares," I said. "I've been trying to decide if I want to stay for Old Hot Crotch's soiree tonight."

"I heard Tony tell her he'd stay for a while."

"Maybe I'll stay for a little while."

"I thought you would," she gibed. "But honestly, I don't think you've got the ghost of a chance."

"Maybe not. But I've got four more weeks to prime the pump."

She raised her eyebrows in twin question marks.

"Last night the Gruesome Twosome asked me to extend my engagement for another four weeks," I said. "So what do you think of that?"

"I think it's super duper," she chortled.

After a while, Aidey came back down the hall. It was plain to see her problem had been solved to her complete satisfaction. She was purring like a Bentley after a good lube job.

"Traaacy!" Out in the hall, Marc's voice rose to an apoplectic pitch. "You're supposed to be doing the clog dance in the jazz number!" he raged.

"Gee, Marc, I'm sorry I missed the number—but it's too late now."

"It's not too late for some heads to roll at option time. I can tell you that."

The picture number was a southern theme. Tony came through the archway in a replica of Rhett Butler's evening attire. He had Clark Gable backed off the map. I gazed at Rhett Butler and imagined that he had just swept me up in his arms and was carrying me up those stairs to force me into that bridal bed. Only I wasn't screeching and kicking in protest like that silly Miss Scarlet.

"How does it look?" he asked self-consciously.

"Very dashing and debonair," I gushed.

Dickie looked him over and sneered, "It looks like home-made shit!"

"Dickie! You impudent brat!" I scolded. "I'm going to tell your father."

"Aw, go piss up a rope!" he said, stomping down the hall toward his room.

Slim pulled the blackout and Tony made his entrance. I shifted my position on the stool so I could see him out on stage.

Tracy gave me a scornful look. "Why didn't you bring your weaving, Penelope?"

"What do you mean?"

"I mean your campaign to ensnare Odysseus is too obvious."

"Is anyone else aware of my wicked web?"

"I'd say Dickie is. He's green-eyed jealous."

As we passed his door, I knocked and called, "Can I come in?"

"I ain't in here!" he stormed.

Later, when I went out for my number, Barry was sitting on one of the stools. He was dressed to the nines.

"You should make the list of the ten best-dressed men," I told him. He was inordinately pleased.

Poor Barry. He had an unslakeable thirst for adulation. That thirst was probably the impetus that made him strive so hard to have people like him.

"Oh yeah," said Slim. "Barry dresses like a fashion plate, but you should've seen him before his wife took him in hand." He spat between his teeth. "He didn't have two rags that matched, his English was atrocious and his manners were worse. He couldn't get across the stage without a road map. Isn't that right, Barry?"

Barry smiled, but there was angry humiliation behind it.

Several times before, I'd noticed that Slim wasn't very fond of Barry. And now, he had deliberately aimed the spotlight behind his elegant facade.

"Yes, Slim, she taught me everything I know about show biz." He tried to sound nonchalant, but he wasn't too successful. It was plain that Slim's pointed expose had mortified his pygmy ego. Underneath the veneer was a mountain of inferiority and a molehill of self-esteem. Maybe that was the reason he sought such low-class trash for companions—in their company he didn't feel inferior.

Slim had stripped away his false front, and although I didn't have a very high opinion of him, I felt sorry for him.

We are all Paliaccis. We all have a raw and vulnerable self that we keep buried behind a many-faceted facade. We let different people see different facets, but we let no one—not even ourselves—see the true self we keep buried there.

Mumbling some inanity, I went to stand in the wings and wait for the blackout.

CHAPTER ELEVEN

That night, after the finale, I took a long time dressing. At a party, I always feel like odd man out.

When I went over to the green room the party was going full blast. And, judging by Luttie's strident cackle, it was going to be a huge success.

She was parading Barry around with a possessive hold on his arm. But while she was staking her claim on him, I noticed her attention kept straying toward the big table. The magnet, of course, was Tony Blake. He was pouring champagne for Darlene.

It was no surprise to find that Old Hot Crotch had her eyeballs peeled for Tony. So did half the females in the theatre.

Stopping to exchange some chit-chat here and there, I made my way to the table. Darlene had already been to the champagne too many times. Especially since she was half-swacked before the show was over.

I sauntered up to the table and held out a paper cup. "My goodness," I cooed. "Luttie certainly hired a handsome bartender for her soiree."

He filled the cup. "She certainly invited some beautiful guests, too." He lifted my hand and kissed my fingers before he put the cup back into my hand.

My heart started beating in waltz time. It was the first time he'd ever given any indication that I wasn't the prop dummy. I pasted a fatuous smile on my face and gave him a flirty glance over the rim of my cup. I realized I was over-doing the scene, but, Shakespeare said, "Bait well the hook; the fish will bite." Fate—and the Gruesome Twosome—had given me a second chance and this time around I vowed to follow his advice. I also vowed to use a mighty potent lure.

There were a lot of other lusciously baited hooks plopping in the pond.

"Jade! Stop flirting with Tony and let him attend to the important things . . . " Darlene held out her cup for a refill. "This is some swell ol' ho . . . ol' Luttie is giving for her loverly doverly. She didn't invite me, but I stayed just to annoy her."

She looked around until she spied Barry and Luttie. She weaved over and said, "Hey Barry . . . wanna dance?"

Luttie glared at her and said, "You were not invited to this party, so why don't you get lost! You drunken slob!"

"Who're you calling a drunken slob? You ugly old trollop!"

Evidently Darlene was drunk enough to challenge Luttie to a choice of swords or pistols under the dueling oak. I didn't want to be her second.

I hated to lose my tenuous hold on Tony's budding gallantry, but I eased my way through the crowd and headed for the stage.

Aidey was sitting on the bench by the radiator— looking like a woebegone baboon. She was casting furtive glances into the green room, no doubt with a morbid desire to see what Luttie and Barry were doing.

"Why, Aidey dear! What are you doing hiding out here in the dark while the man you love is in there letting Luttie put a ring in his nose?" I taunted sweetly. "I saw the message you wrote on his birthday card— the one vowing all your love."

She spit at my heels as I left.

Huey came from behind the backdrop and sat on the bench beside her. I hoped she wouldn't tell him about my nasty remarks. I didn't want Huey to find out that sometimes I was less than a nice person. Safely hidden behind a border, I paused to eavesdrop.

When he saw her hangdog look, he began teasing her with a funny line of chatter. Huey was quite a charming rogue. In a couple of minutes he had her tittering like a school girl.

The chaise lounge I used in my number was still in place. The stagehands must have been too eager to get to the free booze to strike the set. I shoved it further up stage, made myself comfortable and sipped the vinegary champagne. I'd had enough of the party.

A form showed against the faint illumination in the wings. Then I saw it was Tony. Was he merely going to the men's room? Or had he also had enough of the fun and frivolity? Whichever, I would try to recapture his finger-kissing mood.

"If you're going to sneak out," I called softly, "Wait until I get my coat and I'll go with you."

My voice startled him but he turned and came up stage.

"Who won the brannigan?" I asked.

"It looked like a draw." He sat on the foot of the chaise. "No blood was spilled."

"Good. I'd hate to see Darlene get fired."

"I've noticed she and Luttie aren't very friendly."

"That's putting it mildly. For two cents and a brace of pistols, they'd murder each other."

"Are you enjoying the party?" he asked.

"No. I was thinking if the janitor hadn't locked the lobby doors, I'd sneak out through the front."

He raised his cup. "Here's to your undetected getaway." He stood up and yawned. "Goodnight."

Whether it had been the champagne or my fatal charm that had unkinked his neck out at the big table, it's effect was swiftly losing ground.

"Would you like to walk me to my hotel?" I sounded like an ingenue playing a Southern belle.

"Sure, why not?" He sounded like a condescending yankee.

The janitor unlocked the lobby door and let us out into the freezing night.

Sleet and snow had transformed the streets into glistening lanes and the lampposts into spangled minarets. It was a fairy-land and the night elves were bathing the scene in moonglow and stardust. I scarcely dared to breathe for fear of shattering this enchanted illusion.

We walked a long while in silence. He had his hands in his overcoat pockets. Boldly I put my hand in his pocket and snuggled my fingers in his palm.

I was sure Anthony Blake wouldn't care to indulge in a dialogue of backstage gossip, but I had to start a conversation pretty soon or end up merely saying "goodnight."

"Fait accompli," I finally said.

He lifted a questioning eyebrow.

"Luttie's coup de theatre." A bit of peddler's French was usually good for a laugh.

"What was her coup de theatre?"

"The birthday party. That's her way of letting the whole company know Barry Previn is now her personal property."

"He seemed very happy to let her take ownership."

"She might have a bit of trouble. Whycherley says, next to the pleasure of making a new mistress is that of being rid of an old one. I think it'll be kinda hard to be rid of Aidey."

"Aidey?"

"Yeah, that poor neurotic love-sick thing will stick as tight as cuckle burrs on a cow's tail."

He laughed. "You actors . . . you certainly have a novel way of saying things."

"You actors. Was it my imagination, or was there a slight derogatory emphasis on those two words? Oh well, at least my feeble attempt at comedy had gotten a laugh.

"We actors also have a novel way of doing things. You should let us teach you some of the tricks of our trade."

"I'm sure you'd be an excellent teacher. And tonight I'd be more than willing to learn." He squeezed my fingers.

When I had assimilated that remark, I realized he thought I was propositioning him! I felt myself flushing with embarrassment. Then—damn him—I was mad as hell! I hate men who always manage to find an indirect sexual invitation in everything you say.

I jerked my hand out of his pocket. "You have a one-track mind!" I said contemptuously. "I was referring to the acting trade. And believe me *you* certainly could use a lot of them."

He shrugged.

"There's no need for you to walk any further. I'm sorry to destroy your expectations, but I don't play one night stands."

"Then why are you working in a burlesque show?"

This time there was no mistaking the unsavory implication. I felt my hackles rise higher.

"Bad genes and lack of a proper upbringing, no doubt."

"Why do you go out on the stage and take your clothes off for a howling mob of degenerates?"

"It beats dragging a croaker sack through a cotton field." I said flippantly. "And the pay is infinitely better."

At the hotel I said, "Thank you for walking me home. You were charming company."

"I'll see you to the elevator."

"Ah yes, ever the gentleman," I said scornfully. "The Brahman must always observe the proprieties—even with the lower classes." I stood aside to allow him to push the swinging doors for me.

At the elevator he put his hands on my shoulders and turned me to face him. " I'm sorry if I offended you." It sounded like the usual parroted apology.

"You're absolved. I'm used to propositions."

He looked down at me and said," I'm truly sorry."

I lifted my eyes to meet his, and cursed silently. Damn it to hell, why did my brains have to turn into a bowl of mush every time his eyes met mine?

"Just forget it," I said. "I'm not the village virgin. It won't send me into a decline."

As I turned toward the elevator, he let his hands trail downward over my chest. Suddenly he pushed them under my coat, wrapped his arms around me and pulled me savagely against his body.

The heavy buttons were hurting my breasts, but it didn't matter. Nothing mattered as long as I was in his arms. I put my hands on his face and lifted my lips to meet his eager kiss.

It was a kiss of sublime ecstasy. A kiss of passionate surrender. This was my reason for being. And I knew, with a thrill of triumph, that he was feeling the same emotion. He lifted his mouth to murmur endearing words against my lips, then he was kissing me again for what seemed like an eternity of bliss.

Slowly he took his lips from mine and I felt his arms go limp. I opened my eyes—and stared in utter disbelief. The expression on his face was one of scornful aversion. Without a word, he walked swiftly across the lobby and pushed through the doors, disappearing out into the street.

Staring after him, I knew I'd been given a deliberate brush-off. I was fleetingly aware of the smiles of the night clerk and the ancient bellboy. Inside the elevator, I blindly made a jab at the buttons on the panel. The damned thing could go through the roof for all I cared.

I was burning with anger and humiliation. One embrace from him and I had melted like Icarus' wings. I had let him know that I was his for the taking. And he had walked away leaving me feeling like a cheap barstool barfly.

Hot tears kept spilling over as I undressed, took a bath and crawled into bed. I laid there wide awake trying to think of some way to save my pride, and ego. Now I knew why saving face was so vitally important to the Orientals.

Seppuku was out. I didn't have a samurai sword.

The worst humiliation would be having to face him tomorrow.

Should I be coolly aloof? Disdainfully amused? Supremely indifferent—as though passionate love scenes in hotel lobbies were a nightly habit of mine? Or tell the Gruesome Twosome I couldn't extend my engagement and leave at the end of the week?

Leave town? And give him the satisfaction of knowing he was the reason!

Never in a million years!

To hell with that sanctimonious jerk. I wouldn't leave a scratch house in Slumsville for him. Damned stuffed shirt. Damned prissy-assed snob. Lousy amateur. I'd ignore him. That's what I would do.

Which seemed like a perfect solution. Until I realized I didn't want him to ignore me. Not just yet.

Like every other female who has ever been given the brush-off by a man, I wanted to get even. I tried to think of some way I could make him desperately want me again. Just one more time, so I could have the exquisite pleasure of retaliation.

Then I thought of the perfect revenge. If watching me undress on stage whetted his baser desires a trifle, why not force him to watch the whole performance—up close—and whet the hell out of them?

All I had to do was dream up a number in which he would have to be out on the stage with me, while I went slinking around shedding my wardrobe like Salome shedding her veils.

That should even up the score, nicely.

He would be absolutely furious. He would squirm with humiliation over the indignity of having to sit on the stage of a burlesque theatre and be part of a strip number. And I'd make sure that he squirmed with another kind of emotion, also. That would be better than having his head on a platter.

I started searching my brain for an idea. The best one to surface was a Roman garden scene—with me in a sexy costume a la Cleopatra and Mister Anthony Clay Blake, from the old New England family of Blakes, seated in a Roman garden seat, in a costume a la Julius Caesar. And he would have to sit there and sing to me and I would wear my smallest G-string and no pasties.

By the time my brain and I got all the details exactly right, in this wickedly beautiful idea, Cleopatra was falling asleep to dream of sweet revenge.

CHAPTER TWELVE

Next morning it was still a wickedly beautiful idea. All the way to the theatre, I kept filling in elaborate details and happily visualizing Mister Blake's acute embarrassment.

As I hurried across stage behind the curtain I stumbled over Penny. That was nothing unusual, though. Anybody crossing the darkened stage was likely to stumble over Penny.

Penny had stars in her eyes and a dogged ambition that far outstripped her talent. Each morning she came in an hour early and practiced her ballet lessons. But after years of lessons and hundreds of hours of practice, she was still the most wooden dancer in the line.

"I'm sorry, Penny. I didn't see you."

"That's all right. I'm not hurt."

When I finished my morning metamorphosis I underdressed for my number, put on my robe and went down the hall to Barry's office. He was sitting on his spine in the big leather chair with his heels hooked on the edge of the desk.

"I didn't realize you were working so hard," I said. "Or I wouldn't have disturbed you."

"I was thinking real hard about working," he grinned.

"I'd like to do a Cleopatra number next week. I'd like a Roman garden scene with a fancy Roman seat—so Tony can sit out on stage and sing my trailers. And I'd like a fountain to dress it up. Would you have one around anywhere?"

"Yeah we have one. It's in the prop room. Tell Smitty to paint it up to look like marble."

I thanked him and went looking for Smitty. I explained about the number and the props and the fountain and asked if I could go see them.

"It's probably buried somewhere in the prop room." he said. "Let's go look."

The prop room was at the rear of the stage. The door was directly behind the end of the pinrail. It was jammed with debris. At the far end of the long room, halfway between the floor and the ceiling, a wide platform went from wall to wall. Over on the left side, a straight up and down ladder was nailed to the front edge. It looked like an old talfat—a ledge where children slept in small farm houses.

While Smitty moved some big things around looking for the fountain, I gazed at the assortment of things on the storage platform. It was dimly lit back there but I could make out lamps, chairs, and a reproduction settee. At the very edge, looking as though it would fall any minute, was the inevitable prop dummy.

"Hey, Smitty. You'd better climb up on the shelf and secure your prop dummy. It looks like it's going to fall."

"We haven't got a prop dummy. We loaned it to some high school kids for one of their plays."

"They must've brought it back. It's up there on the platform and it's going to fall."

Smitty came from behind the old Gezeeka box and stared back at the platform. "What the hell is that?" He pulled a chain hanging from the ceiling and flooded the room with bright light. "Oh, my God . . . it can't be!" he gasped.

Then I saw what was there on the edge of the platform. Smitty's hand over my mouth stifled my scream, but nothing could tear my eyes away from the horror that lay on the platform with its head lolling over the edge.

Aidey had been ugly in life. In death, she was hideous. Her bloated face was the color of an eggplant. The perfect white teeth stood out starkly against the purple tongue that protruded between them. Knotted around her throat was a length of trickline with one long end dangling off the edge. Her heavy black hair spilled over the edge along with the rope. Part of a crocheted shawl showed beneath an outflung arm.

I twisted out of Smitty's grasp and ran toward the door. He caught me before I could open it. "Let me go!" My voice rose to hysterical shrillness. He grabbed my shoulders and shook, hard.

"Don't you realize you can't go running out there screaming that Aidey had been murdered? In ten seconds, this place would be a madhouse!"

"We have to tell somebody. We can't leave her up there," I said. "What are we going to do?"

"I don't know . . . I don't know. I'd better call Huey back here . . . tell him what happened. He's the manager, let him handle it." Neither one of us looked back at the platform.

I heard my fanfare being played. He propelled me through the door and held onto me while he secured the padlock. "Don't say anything. Try to act natural," he pleaded.

I ran down stage, pushed my way through a crowd and walked out on stage in my robe. There were surprised gasps behind me and startled faces peering from the wings.

Despite the numbness in my head, I paraded through my number. When it was finally over and I came off stage, Smitty was explaining to Huey and Barry, "We were looking for the props she wanted. All of a sudden she said she felt faint. Before I could get the ammonia capsules out of the emergency kit, she just folded up. I finally brought her around with the ammonia.

Then she heard her music and went running out before I could stop her."

I didn't have to put on an act to back up his story. I was in a state of weak-kneed shock.

Huey put his arm around me. "You'd better go inside and lie down." My knees buckled as I sank down on the daybed.

"Do you want me to call a doctor?"

"Smitty . . . haven't you told him?"

"No. There were too many people around. I just said you'd fainted. It was the only explanation I could think of."

"Explanation for what?" Huey sounded annoyed. "If she didn't faint, then what's this all about?"

Smitty told him as calmly as he could.

"Mother of God!" Huey exclaimed. "Aidey murdered? Who could've done such a horrible thing?" He looked dazed. "We'll have to call the police . . . they'll want to talk to you and Jade before the others find out."

"How can you bring them back here without letting everybody know what happened?"

Huey looked stymied for a moment. Then he said, "I'll tell them that Jade saw an accident this morning and the police want to get a statement from her."

As Huey went out, Tracy eased through the door with a small bottle in her hand. She poured a dollop in a cup and said, "Here drink this; it'll revive you in ten seconds."

"What is it?"

"It's whatever Darlene hid behind her mirror." She sniffed the bottle. "It smells like Darlene's breath, so it's got to be potent."

"I'd better not. I wouldn't want to be giddy when they get here. I'll probably have hysterics as soon as they start asking me questions."

"They?" She smiled. "Is Huey going to call a team of doctors just for a little fainting spell?"

"I didn't faint. You may as well tell her, Smitty. She'll have to find it out."

"Find out what?"

When Smitty told her, she folded into the chair. Under her bright red feathered hat, her face was blank with shock.

"Aidey? Aidey . . . Who would want to murder her?"

He shook his head. "Only God knows who or why, but somebody wound a rope around her neck. She's in the prop room, up on the storage platform. Don't mention it to anyone, Trace." He looked at me. "One hysterical woman is enough." He urged her toward the door. "The overture is on. You're in the opening." And Tracy, who never drank alcohol, drained the contents of the glass.

They left and I leaned back against the pillows and tried to relax. But questions about that awful horror scene in the prop room started niggling at my thoughts. How had the murderer gotten Aidey up that ladder? The platform was at least eight feet above the floor. It would be impossible to climb that ladder without using both hands. I tried to think who would be strong enough to climb up the ladder with a hundred and fifty pounds balanced on his shoulder.

Then another thought occurred. One that was more logical. No one could be carried her up there, but someone could've lured her up there. She could have climbed up there to keep a tryst in a place where there'd be no chance of being surprised. But with whom? And what would be the motive for her murder?

Had she become a threat to Barry? She was a sly conniving bitch, goaded by a morbid desire to marry him. She'd been cunning enough to try to instigate a showdown with Luttie, by pretending to have a secret. Did she intimate it was about Barry?

Or had Luttie given him an ultimatum? Either quit mucking around with Aidey or she'll break off their romance. That would make Aidey a double threat.

An image of her up on that platform floated through my mind. I realized she was still in the gray flowered feed sack she'd worn at the party last night. That meant she'd never left the theatre.

A tap on my door jarred me out of my mental sleuthing. I called, "Come in," and was amazed when Tony walked in.

"I'm sorry you're not feeling well . . ." He was hesitant and ill at ease. "Is there anything I can do?"

"Yes. You can get the hell out of here."

He backed toward the door. "Jade . . . about last night . . . I"m sorry. . ."

"Sorry? Sorry for what? Sorry you lost control of your exalted emotions?" I sneered. "You remind me of a preacher in a whore house—all torn up between your sanctimonious principles and your scorching pants. You make me sick. Get out of here!" Hot tears were stinging my eyes.

The door had hardly closed when there was another knock and Huey came in followed by two large blocks of animated granite. They looked as if both had been carved from the same boulder, except for the small moustache the sculptor had put on one.

"These are the men from homicide, Jade. They want to ask you some questions while we're waiting for the show to break." He went out and closed the door.

One of the coldest temperatures ever recorded was one hundred and twenty-seven degrees below zero. Obviously whoever recorded it had never measured the iciness in a policeman's eyes.

When I was a very small girl, a farmer drove his team of horses down our lane. Before I could scurry inside the gate, he reined them within a scant three feet from my toes. I stood there petrified with terror, unable to move, even though I was certain on of those monsters would lift a great iron-shod hoof and mash me into the ground where no one would ever see me again.

The team by the door gave me the same feeling.

They regarded me as something that escaped from a low-class bawdy house that only employed feebleminded doxies.

"I'm sorry I only have one chair," I apologized.

"You found the body?" asked the moustache.

"Yes, Smitty and I did."

They pushed their hats back and unbuttoned their overcoats.

"Where?"

"On the storage platform at the back of the prop room."

"What can you tell us about the dead girl?" His voice was cold enough to bend steel.

"I don't know anything about her."

"Nothing at all?"

"No. Only from seeing her around the theatre."

The other one hadn't opened his granite mouth. Apparently his sole duty was to stare a hole through the center of my head. My inquisitor gave him a nod and he got into the act.

"Did she play around with any of the men in the theatre?"

"How should I know? I didn't follow her around."

"How long you been here?"

"Four weeks."

"In four weeks you must've noticed something about her." He insisted." What kind of a girl was she? What was she like?"

"She was a smarmy little damsel-in-distress."

"What do you mean?"

She was about as helpless as a hungry lion, but she had a teary-eyed helpless little girl routine that she performed with the skill of a Bernhardt."

"Was she an attractive girl?"

"She made a baboon look good."

"Any other outstanding points?" he asked with heavy sarcasm.

I decided I'd better bridle my tongue. Being on the defensive definitely wasn't the way to win points with the two official gentlemen.

"Did you like the girl?"

"No! She was a phony sniveling creep and I couldn't stand her," I said, before I could get the bridle in place.

"Were you jealous of her?"

"Holy Christ, no!"

"Then why were you giving her a bad time last night by being sarcastic and nasty to her?"

Unpleasant surprise left my mouth hanging open. Last night while Huey sat on the bench with her, she'd obviously told him about how nasty I'd been.

And Huey had lost no time in passing the information along to my two granite friends. But why was he in such a hurry to tell them? There were no rubber hose marks on him. Besides, I thought he liked me.

"I don't know," I faltered. "I was just being nasty."

"What were you being nasty about?"

Thank heaven, she hadn't told him I was needling her about Barry. But naturally she would leave that part out. She would never reveal anything about her scheming tricks.

"I don't remember." I lied. "I despised her, so I was just trying to annoy her."

"Did you despise her enough to want to see her dead?"

"No, of course not."

That question gave me a jolt of apprehension. Were those oblique questions designed to find motive for murder?

The police, like Delilah Laine's silicon implants, could make mountains out of molehills. I tried a detracting tactic.

I put my foot on the shelf bracket, tilted the chair back and let them have a glimpse of my shapely leg. Ha. I would've fared as well with the gentlemen on Mount Rushmore.

"How about the other people in the theatre—did any of them despise her?"

I was saved from answering when Barry tapped on the door and came in. He stared at the two in surprise, then smiled and said. "Good morning." They ignored him.

"Can you do your number, Jade?" he asked. "Or shall I have one of the girls take your spot?"

"I'm all right. I can do it."

I smiled at my two unwelcome guests and said, "You gentlemen will have to excuse me while I get dressed for my number."

They went out and I leaned against the closed door and breathed a sigh of relief.

"I saw Huey bring them in—what did they want?"

"They're policemen."

"Anybody could tell that as soon as they saw them," he said wryly. "Even Dickie would never mistake them for visiting uncles."

He cocked an inquiring eyebrow. "Were they going to arrest you for fainting?"

"I didn't faint. Smitty was stalling for time." I figured I may as well tell him the truth. "They're here about Aidey."

"Aidey? What about Aidey?" Barry asked in puzzled surprise.

I wondered what kind of reaction my next words would get.

"She's been murdered. Smitty and I found her in the prop room when we went to look for the fountain." I shouldn't have been so blunt.

The color drained out of his face so swiftly, I thought he was going to faint.

He stared at me in absolute disbelief. "Aidey . . . murdered. Why . . . Who . . . ?" His voice dwindled away.

"I'm sorry Barry. I shouldn't have blurted it out like that. But I wanted to tell you before you heard it from them."

He sank down in my chair, put his head on his arms and dissolved into wracking sobs. Was it shock? Grief? Guilt? Remorse? I couldn't tell, but whatever the reason I was glad I'd kept the police from seeing his first reaction.

I put a dampened towel in his hand. "You'd better get control of yourself. If they see you like this, it might arouse some nasty suspicions."

"Thanks, Jade." He blotted at the tears. "Why would anyone murder Aidey? She was the sweetest, most wonderful girl in the world." He sobbed.

I didn't share his sentiments and I couldn't feel any sympathy for his grief—but the devil takes care of his own. And so do actors. No matter how much one actor dislikes another, he'll always be on their side against the law.

"Please don't let them know I put you on your guard."

"Thanks again, Jade."

He went out. I sat in my chair and tried to relax and calm my twisting nerves. It was a hopeless try. As I studied my drawn face in the mirror, nine little migraine devils on red hot hooves came marching up behind my right ear. They stomped over my head, circled my right eye—then bored their way in through the socket and started beating out the Anvil Chorus inside my skull.

CHAPTER THIRTEEN

Out on stage, the two detectives were leaning against the pinrail talking to Huey. Dickie was eavesdropping.

There was a mild undercurrent of curiosity buzzing around.

Mimi stopped and asked, "Was anybody hurt?"

I drew a blank. "Hurt?"

"I heard Huey tell Slim you saw an accident and those two detectives wanted to question you about it."

"Oh, that. Two drunks smashed up their fenders."

"Imagine being questioned by the police just for that."

"Yeah, isn't it silly?"

Darlene was standing at the other end of the pinrail regarding the two detectives with a puzzled frown. I motioned to Tracy. "I know we're supposed to keep quiet, but I think we'd better tell Darlene."

"Absolutely," said Tracy. "After a couple of her morning eye-openers, she is unpredictable. She might get too eager to help out in the investigation."

We sauntered past the two detectives, who were discussing baseball with Huey. Aidey was just another statistic to them. I wondered what their names were. Having a name would make them seem like humans.

"We have something to tell you," said Tracy. "We're not supposed to know about it, but as soon as the show is over everybody will know."

"My God!" Darlene gazed at the detectives with feigned dismay. "Are they going to raid the joint?"

It's worse than that. And please try to control yourself."

"Did somebody get murdered?" She asked in mock horror.

When Tracy told her, she gazed at the prop room door in genuine horror. "I was only clowning!" she gasped. "I never . . . dreamed anything like that could be true . . . I was just clowning. Who'd want to murder her? That . . . big . . . weirdo. . ."

"You're always just clowning. You'd better start sobering up, and you'd better start right now. When the police start asking questions, don't go spouting off about what a creep she was and how much you hated her. They might think all that hatred could be a motive for murder."

"Trace, don't say that!" she cried. "I couldn't kill anybody . . . you know I couldn't!"

My fanfare started and I ran for the stage. All the way through the number, I kept wishing I hadn't spouted off about how much I disliked her. My two granite friends seemed to think anything short of brotherly love was an excellent motive for murder.

The finale curtain came down and the cast started moving off stage. Suddenly there was a commotion as Dickie came battling his way through the crowd, shouting for his father.

"Tramp! Tramp! There's a whole bunch of cops in the green room. There mus' be a hunnert of 'em!"

Before anyone could react to this startling announcement, the two detectives heaved their weight from against the pinrail and herded the people together—and in blunt police parlance told them about the murder.

Actors are such volatile creatures I expected pandemonium. Instead they were stunned into awestruck silence.

The moustacheless one held up his hand for attention.

"Don't anybody leave this area. As soon as you are dressed my partner and I will be asking you some questions." He had an afterthought. "I'm Lieutenant Mulchahe. This is Sergeant O'Brien," he said looking us over. His expression plainly said, in all his years, he'd never seen a human menagerie that revolted him more then we did.

"O'Brien, go around and get their names while they get dressed. It'll save time."

"Lieutenant, is it necessary for everybody to stay?" asked Barry. "Couldn't half go out now and when they come back the other half could go? Otherwise they'll have to work all day long on coffee and doughnuts."

Mulchahe tromped the stiffness out of his legs. "Let's get this clear. When a murder has been committed, no one leaves the scene." He looked around. "Some vital piece of evidence could be removed if people were allowed to run in and out."

I gave in to my fatal affliction—the inability to keep my mouth shut. "The murder was committed last night." I said. "If anyone had any incriminating evidence to hide, they'd have removed it last night. And I'm sure they wouldn't bring it back with them this morning."

He regarded me with as much expression as a stage brace.

"How do you know she was murdered last night?" He bore down heavy on the word you.

"She still has on the dress she wore for the party."

"What party?"

"It was my birthday party," explained Barry.

"Did everybody stay for the party?"

"No. Not even half of them."

"O'Brien, write down the names of the ones that stayed."

Tracy looked toward the side steps and grated, "Here comes Old Hot Crotch! I hope they don't judge us by the way she acts."

Luttie did a large double-take when she saw the detectives. She pranced over, planted herself in front of them and began to seesaw her pelvis from side to side while she leered up at them like a wall-eyed frog.

"Gee whiz. I ain't never been in a raid, but I'm willin' to cooperate." She was doing her Mae West bit. "You boys see that I get my picture in the paper and I'll let you come up and see me sometime." She pulled her face awry and *crk crked* her tongue against her jaw teeth.

"Why can't she shut up?" Tracy said between clinched teeth. "Hasn't she got any brains?"

"It doesn't require any brains to be an idiot."

"She doesn't know what a silly bitch she really is."

"I'd say the Lieutenant does." He was regarding her with the expression of a man who had just found a large larva floating in his soup.

Apparently it began to seep through her piss-ant brain that her act wasn't going over too well. But she gave it another try.

"What's the matter?" she lipped. "Has everybody lost their sense of humor?" She stretched her neck up and looked around. "If we're holding a wake, where's the body laid out?"

Barry told her what had happened.

The emotional reaction was way overdone and the weeping and wailing smelled strongly of ham rind.

The coroner came with the men from the morgue. Smitty unlocked the prop room door for them and the two granite statues.

"Tracy, where's Darlene?"

"Probably in her room getting paralyzed. If she is, she'll be a menace by the time they question her. The drunker she gets, the more bitterness she gives out about Luttie and Barry."

We found her in her room, looking cold sober. Tracy began laying down the law. Stay sober. Keep your mouth shut. Don't mention the backstage romantic triangle—it would stir up a scandal—and God knows we don't need that! Don't mention the hole under the sink. I suspected she wanted to keep the lines of secret communication open.

"I haven't got a drop, Trace. I swear. I only had enough for one little drink this morning."

"Okay, kid, I believe you."

As we were coming back down the stairs she said, "Have you been thinking the same thing I have?"

"If you mean casting Barry Previn as the prime suspect, I guess I have."

"Who else would have any reason to get rid of her?"

"Nobody that I can think of. Maybe Luttie. Maybe both of them. Aidey was beginning to be a mighty long thorn in the side of their plans. But let's keep our opinions to ourselves. I wouldn't want Barry to be suspected because we couldn't keep our mouths shut."

"Don't worry about us. It's some of the other people here who're going to be dropping a lot of hints." She went on down the hall to her room.

Royal Rydeen was sitting in the chair by my door. He held my hand and told me the coroner and the men from the morgue had gone and taken the dreadful burden from the prop room with them.

"What else is happening?"

"The two cops have set up headquarters in Barry's office. They're taking the cast in one at a time for questioning."

"I think I need a cup of hot tea."

When I went out onstage, the lights were full up and the front curtain was open. Two uniformed policemen were standing on the apron. No doubt to keep anyone from escaping over the footlights.

Luttie was standing with them, being her usual obnoxious self. She was expounding on her vast knowledge of the theatre. According to her, she was the complete authority on the art from the Greek Tragedies on down to the Chautauquas.

Tony and Caralyn were sitting on the chaise lounge. She

looked at me and said, "Oh, Jade, how awful for you. It must have been terribly shocking."

"Please let's not talk about it." Somehow they had become outsiders. They worked in the show, but they were not one of us.

When I came back across the stage, they were still there. I didn't even glance at Tony. Him and his damned ancestors!

With a cup of tea in each hand, I kicked lightly on Tracy's door. Darlene was there looking like the morning after. Maybe Tracy should have looked closer for her hidden bottle.

"Have you heard anything new?" I asked.

"No. Nothing."

"Who's in there now?"

"The bereaved girl friend."

"Has she solved the case for them?"

"I didn't even bother to listen."

"Those cops won't pay any attention to what that wind-sucking jerk blows out." said Darlene.

"Let's go to my dressing room," I said. "We'll leave the door open so we can see what's going on."

It paid off. The door of the office opened and Luttie oozed through, like an oversexed jellyfish with St. Vitus dance. She seesawed and gyrated as she flung one-liners back into the room to devastate the cops with her witty repartee.

Tracy watched her exaggerated mugging and said, "How did she manage to miss evolution?"

The Gruesome Twosome finally arrived. Evidently they knew what string to pull. In a very short time, Mulchahe received a phone call and then announced everybody could go out for dinner, but it was too late. It was almost time for the curtain to go up.

The show was ragged and wooden. The actors went through the scenes like automatons.

When it was over, Mulchahe called everybody out on stage and laid down a lot of orders. He finished by stressing that he wanted everybody in the theatre an hour early tomorrow morning.

CHAPTER FOURTEEN

As soon as I awoke, I called the desk and had the morning papers sent up. GIRL MURDERED IN BURLESQUE THEATRE, screamed the headlines in the leading daily. GIRL GARROTED AFTER DRUNKEN BRAWL IN BURLESQUE THEATRE, said another one.

Each paper tried to outdo the other in depicting the awful depravity of the denizens of burlesque. There were pictures of the theatre and close-ups of the pictures in the lobby. A small snapshot of Aidey was lost in the over-smear. All of which would make getting into the theatre a very unpleasant experience. There would be swarms of reporters and the vultures that always circle around a murder scene.

There were two uniformed policemen stationed at the stage door. They held back the crowd and let us through. But nothing could hold back the filthy obscenities that the women in the crowd hurled at each girl as she arrived at the stage door.

More members of the better element, of course.

Marc and Tony were in the hall having a pointed discussion. As I passed them, I raised a questioning eyebrow at Marc.

"Tony is upset because he had to come in early. I've been trying to tell him it's nothing personal. All of us had to come in early."

"I don't like being treated like a common criminal!" Tony burst out angrily. "And I don't like not being allowed to leave."

"Tony turned in his notice, but the detectives told him nobody would be allowed to leave the company until the case was solved." explained Marc.

"We all feel so terribly sorry for Mister Blake," I said. "But it looks like he'll have to be stuck here in this den of low class humanity for quite a while, doesn't it?"

Dickie, as usual, had commandeered the chair beside my door; from which he could greet—or heckle—the morning arrival of each actor. His morning was always a huge success if he could annoy Tony.

"Hey Tony!" he yelled. "You couldn't leave now, nohow. Marc's got a swell new number he wants you to sing. Wanna hear how it goes?"

Dickie knew umpteen verses of a sad saga about a gal that was hooked on cocaine. He patted the air with his foot to keep time and began to sing.

> She wuz walkin' down Broadway, turned off Main
> Lookin' for a spot to buy cocaine.
> She needed a sniff—a sniff of big C
> So I gived her a sniff on me.

> First time I saw her, she wuz perched on the steeple
> With her rump in the air to accommodate the people
> Honey have a sniff—have a sniff on me
> Honey have a sniff on me

Las' time I saw her, she was floating down the river
With the birds and the bees afeedin' on her liver
Honey have a sniff—have a sniff on me
Honey have a sniff on me.

Mark thought it was funny, but Tony glared at him in high disgust and went to his dressing room.

"Chalk one up for Dirty Dickie." I pretended to applaud.

"Aw, he thinks he's bettern we are. I wisht he would leave." He curled his lip. "I don't like him worth shit."

Chou Chou came in a pace in front of Darlene. Losing an hour's sleep had left him in a foul mood, but he was as meticulously gotup as usual. "Now that we're here an hour early—what the hell are we supposed to do?"

"Answer the same questions we answered yesterday," said Darlene. Under the bright scarf hiding her curlers, her face looked gray and sallow and her breath was sour enough to pucker the Mona Lisa's smile.

Barry Previn came in showing signs of strain. His hand shook as he took a sip of his coffee.

"He looks like he was slaving over a hot crotch all night," observed Darlene.

Bryce clasped Barry's hand, then put his arm around his shoulders and gave him a buck-up hug.

Bryce's pawing over Barry didn't surprise me.

The first time I saw him I thought he was a closet queen. The morning I walked into the wardrobe room and saw him soul-kissing the beautiful chorus boy who had such sexy dark eyes and a mop of black curls, I was sure of it. It might be Damon and Pythias with Barry, but with Brycie girl it was pure homoeroticism.

Royal Rydeen joined the group. Without his greasepaint and rouge, he looked ten years older than he actually was.

Chou Chou looked at his watch. "I hope to hell they're not going to drag us down here early every morning." He made it sound like a death sentence.

"Yeah," said one of the featherbrained Boys. "Why don't those big old girls just arrest the murderer and get this silly business over with?"

"Which one of us would you have them arrest?" asked Marc sarcastically.

"Which one of *us* . . . " exploded Chou Chou. "Just what the hell do you mean by *one of us*?"

"It shouldn't be too hard to figure out." Mulchahe loomed in the archway from the stage. "It means one of you people back here is a murderer," he stated with brutal frankness.

There were shocked gasps as each of us stared at the other faces—desperately denying that the accusation was meant for us.

"My God! He's right!" said Delilah Laine. She surveyed us from her end of the hall as though she'd never seen one of us before in her entire life. "It had to be one of you. No stranger could get back here."

As jarring as those two thunderbolts had been I knew both Mulchahe and Delilah had to be right. A stranger would have the same chance of being unobserved back here as Paul Bunyan and his great blue ox, Babe.

Marc glared down the hall. "One of us, Miss Laine?" There was large surprise in his words. "I was under the unfavorable impression that you also worked back here."

"I couldn't have killed her," said Miss Laine. "I didn't even know which one she was." She went inside and shut the door.

Tracy glanced around. "Where's the bereaved girlfriend?"

"She'll be here any minute, spouting all those crocodile tears," said Darlene. "She must have geysers for tear ducts."

Strangely enough, despite Mulchahe's order, Luttie didn't show up for the matinee. But she made up for the absence with a never-to-be-forgotten prelude to the evening performance.

Some of the musicians had come up to have a smoke before the show. The smoke was choking me; but I left the door open, because Tony was leaning against the newel post arguing the pros and cons of classical music with the musicians. He was one of the strongest on the pro side.

I told myself I hated him . . . Myself told me I was a liar.

Luttie came in from the stage. Seeing a group of men, she pranced over and bellied her way into their midst. With her usual rutting familiarity, she hooked her hand through Tony's arm and allied herself on his side. She professed a predilection for the music of Johann Sebastian Bach. Could be. But somehow I was absolutely sure that her idea of a prick song had nothing to do with counterpoint.

As she talked, she flicked a long red tongue in and out. A movement as obscene as it was significant. She squeezed her little flabby dugs against his arm and eyed the front of his pants like a hungry coyote eyeing a plump chicken.

Tony let her hand drop and said he was going to the green room for coffee.

"I think you're wasting your time there, Luttie," said the sax man. "I'd say you're not his type."

"I'm every man's type as long as I've got this." She did a grind and patted her pelvis. Then went seesawing off down the hall.

It was easy to see what had raised her sluttishness to a notch higher than usual. She had that glassy-eyed stare, with the widely dilated pupils, that spelled marijuana. She was higher than a Georgia pine tree.

The group shifted. Some left and others came in to have a puff or two. I left the door open, hoping Tony would come back.

The backstage phone was on the wall to the right of the archway. When it rang, whoever was nearest always answered. It jangled and Tracy lifted the receiver. "It's for Luttie. Anybody know where she went?"

"She went down the hall," said Royal. "She probably went in Barry's office."

Tracy went to the far end of the hall and tapped on the door. There was no answer, so she rapped a bit louder. When there was still no answer, she turned the handle and pushed the door open.

No wonder they hadn't heard the knocking.

They wouldn't have heard Gabriel blowing his trumpet!

Barry was lying back in the big leather chair. His belt was unfastened and his zipper was down. Luttie was on her knees between his legs. His eyes were closed and he had both hands wound in her hair helping her pump her head up and down.

For a stunned moment, there was the kind of silence you could drive a herd of buffalo through and never hear a hoofbeat.

Then Tracy said loudly, "When you get through, Luttie, be sure to wipe your chin—you're wanted on the phone."

Barry's eyes flew open to the horrifying realization that their act was playing to a very wide-eyed audience.

Tracy reached in, caught the handle and closed the door. She came back to the phone, picked up the receiver and said, "Luttie can't talk right now. She's got her mouth full."

"Jesus Christ!" said Smitty. "We all know Previn ain't too bright—but you'd think he'd at least have enough brains to lock the door when she's going to give him a blow job!"

"Barry's brains hang between his legs," said Royal. "When Luttie shows up with a hot crotch and a smoking tongue, he just naturally gets hardening of the brain."

No one was surprised when Luttie didn't come out for her phone call.

On intermission, Tracy came around with a tin cup and said she was taking up a collection.

"What for?" somebody asked.

"It's for Luttie," she explained. "We're going to buy her a nice soft cushion, so she won't get calluses on her knees."

"What about the ones on her tongue?" inquired Smitty.

"Slim spat between his teeth. "That little whore has been screwed so many times she's got calluses in her hole."

"Oh, for Christ sake!" flipped Mark. "Who cares? Her hole is her own! She can shovel coal in it if she wants to!"

"Oh, my God!" shrieked Tracy. "Don't tell her! Don't tell her—or she'll be down in the coal bin trying to do it!"

Barry and his little fellatio artist stayed in his office the rest of the evening. I wondered if he could brazen out the jibes and slickers when he had to face people the next morning.

To everyone's surprise, Luttie made herself scarce for the next couple of days. When she did come backstage, Darlene would sing a very lewd version of, "Blow the man down, Babe, blow the man down."

One morning I found Tracy and Darlene at the coffee urn. Tracy was forcing black coffee down Darlene while she lectured her on the evils of drinking.

Darlene looked at me and said piously, "Trace missed her calling. She should have gone into the ministry."

Tracy handed me a cup of tea and we went across the stage. Darlene hurried up the stairs.

"She looked a mite green around the gills," I said. "Maybe you should go see about her."

"Don't worry, her head won't fall off. It never has."

Marc came tearing down the stairs from the men's room. "Tracy for God Almighty sake, will you go up there and see about Darlene? It sounds like she's throwing up her guts!" He invoked heaven for strength. "Always something. Never a dull moment!"

A stagehand was standing by the sand tub. "Well you know that old song, Mark."

"That old song?"

"There's no business like show business."

"Whoever would call this turkey a show?"

"Ah, come on, Marc . . . this is a good show."

"Then shove it up your ass, a good thing never hurt nobody!"

BOOK FOUR

Anthony Clay Blake

I love and I hate
Perhaps you ask me why I do so.
I do not know, but I feel it,
And I am in torment.

CATULLUS, Odes

CHAPTER FIFTEEN

The days immediately following Aidey Wojosky's murder were filled with a sense of dread. Even after the first wave of fear had subsided, there was still a lot of unease among the people—especially the women. None of them would go to the basement by themselves and the chorus girls would not sit alone in their dressing rooms.

My dread was the dread of publicity. If it ever became known that I was working in a burlesque theatre when a lurid murder had been committed, I could never live down the stigma. I hotly resented not being allowed to leave the show.

The police had been there every day with their interrogations. Being treated like the actors and subjected to the same humiliating questions, filled me with an impotent rage.

The newspapers were writing editorials denouncing burlesque as a blight on the city and demanding the closing of all such dives. Since the articles reinforced my own opinions, I fully agreed with them.

Jade heard me voicing my approval of the articles and my opinion of burlesque and the people who worked in it.

"My, what an accurate assessment," she said, with amazed admiration. "You astonish me. I can't imagine how you ever acquired such a clear insight into the depth of our character in such a short space of time. You must be clairvoyant! She assumed an air of total agreement. "No wonder you want to get away from this place and it's low class people."

I wanted to get away from the place, because most of all I wanted to get away from her. I could no longer refuse to admit that I wanted her more than I'd ever wanted any woman. And, even though she set my body on fire, I knew I would never allow myself to become involved with her.

Today was another opening day—and a new low in having to degrade myself. She had dreamed up a Roman number. One where I had to sit out on the stage, half naked in a Roman tunic, and sing to her while she glided around disrobing and dropping the pieces of her costume at my feet. She always came close enough to be sure I would be in the full glare of the spotlight.

But first had come the fiasco of my initial acting attempt.

Marc and Barry had decided it was time I started working in the scenes. Saturday matinee had been my acting debut.

In the scene, Tracy was an editor. I was the star reporter. I was supposed to rush onstage shouting, "Stop the presses! I have the hottest scoop of the year!" Tracy's answer was, "Great, what is it?" Unfortunately, I forgot the follow-up lines. So I went back to waving my arms and shouting about my hot news—until Slim pulled the blackout.

Going offstage, she had both hands over her mouth to stifle a fit of laughter.

"What's so funny?" I asked.

"You. You and your dramatic acting. You looked like you were trying to flag down a fast express train before it made mincemeat of Little Nell out there, tied on the railroad track."

"Maybe you'd better get someone else to do the scene." I said disgustedly. "They're all stupid and degrading anyway."

She turned to face me, her laughter instantly gone.

"Look, you're not the first amateur who ever went out on a stage and made an ass out of himself. And you won't be the last. So why don't you forget about your obnoxious superiority and try to learn something about what you're getting paid to do? You damned overbearing middle-class snob!" She snatched the papers out of my hands and was gone.

I felt about three feet tall as I pushed my way through the giggling jury in the wings.

That night, I was standing by the stairway, waiting for the evening catastrophe to begin, when Royal Rydeen came sauntering down the hall and stopped before Jade's door.

Royal was an aging Lothario whose charm could be turned on and off like a whimsical spigot. He was like a rutting tom cat, always on the prowl for a new female. It was easy to see he had Jade marked for his next conquest. Every night on the break, he would head for her door like a homing pigeon winging its way back to a sex-baited loft.

Tonight he had a long stemmed white rose in his hand. While he waited, he shifted it from hand to hand. When she opened the door, he did a boyish little half bow and held out the rose.

"A white rose for a scarlet lady—each a thing of exquisite loveliness."

I must have groaned.

My contempt for his avocation turned into a grudging admiration for his technique. Instinctively he'd known the psychology of offering her the duel symbol—the white rose of purity, while he designated her the essence of man's desire—the blood red rose of lust. The masterstroke was the subtlety of the paradox. She thanked him, then smiled winsomely and closed the door.

Had I thought she would invite him in?

Anina came down the stairs and Royal shifted his sights. Before he could shift the charm, Chou Chou came in from the stage.

"I was looking for you, Anina," he said. I'm going to do Rain next week. Will you do Tondelayo for me?"

"Sure, Chou Chou."

He gave her a script and showed her where to read. When she finished, he said, "No, honey, you're reading it all wrong."

I was amused by the idea that there could be a right or a wrong way to read one of the tawdry little scenes.

He read the same words back to her and like magic they had a different meaning. His reading changed the whole concept of her lines.

"I'll get it right, Chou Chou," she said. "I just need to go over it a few more times with you."

"We'll rehearse after the show."

I went out on the stage, silently rehearsing my bits of dialogue and wondering why I had ever imagined the art of acting was an insignificant accomplishment.

Later I was standing in the wings in my asinine Mark Anthony get-up, waiting for the number to go on. I was hoping I could get through the ordeal without her seeing my humiliation. Which I was sure she had counted on. Out in that setting, under the colored lights, I felt like I was part of an obscene sexual orgy being performed for a mob of perverts.

She came out in her Cleopatra costume and stopped to speak to Barry Previn. "Would you do me a favor?" she asked in her low honey-splashed voice.

"Want me to kill the poison asp?"

"Oh, no. I need him."

"I'm at your service, O Great Queen Cleopatra," he said, bowing with a deep flourish. "Your wish is my command."

"I demand you to move that barge thing a bit further out on stage, so the audience can see me descending."

He moved the prop where she wanted it. I sat down in that damned seat. Slim flipped a switch and the side spots lighted the stage in a violet glow. The band played the fanfare and Barry made the announcement.

The curtains opened slowly to reveal her seated on a lounge in a seductive pose. Without moving she gave the illusion that every curve of her body was eagerly awaiting a lover. The music from the horns flowed out liquid all soft and I began singing.

She stood up in a flowing movement and stepped down onto the stage. Then she began weaving across the stage in a slow sensuous dance. Cleopatra had begun seducing Mark Anthony.

At the end of the first trailer, the heavily beaded costume seemed to melt onto the floor at my feet, leaving her with a wisp of net for a brassiere and a panel of silk around her hips.

The applause died down and the tempo of the music changed. This time her dancing was a ballet of sexy gyrations—each one bringing her closer to me. I watched her, compelled by the sheer force of her sexuality. Pausing in a pool of amber light close beside the Roman seat, she curled her hands around her bare thighs and drew them slowly, tantalizingly up her sides and cupped them under the full firm breasts . . . Then held them invitingly toward me. The warm feeling in my groins deepened to a burning throb. Watching her dance opened the cellar doors of my mind, but I was powerless to turn my eyes away.

At the end, she put her foot on the edge of the Roman seat, leaned forward and rippled her fingers up her leg, then unsnapped the panels and trailed them across my bare legs.

She removed the brassiere and ran down stage, holding it above her head like a banner. The applause was deafening.

In a blind rush I got out of the costume and into my street clothes. Then I was hearing the stage door slam behind me. The icy air stung my face and cooled my burning temples, but a thousand devils of desire still tended the fiery coals in my belly.

Damn her! I raged as I walked blindly through the frozen slush. Damn her and her lewd immoral dancing!

In the next block, I saw a girl cross under the street light ahead of me. Recognizing Anina's skimming walk, I called her name and she turned to wait for me.

"Would you like to have night lunch with me?" I asked.

"Yes, I would," she said without the coyness of waiting to be coaxed.

"Where would you like to go?" I said. Although I didn't care. I only wanted to delay going to my empty room.

"Let's get a pizza. Angelo makes super ones."

Angelo's facade was in need of a renovation and the windows could have done with a washing. The door squeaked loudly as I followed her in. We found our way to an empty booth. When the waiter came, I ordered a pizza and a bottle of wine.

Anina unwound a bright scarf from her hair and let her coat drop back from her shoulders. Her face glowed with the cold and, for the first time, I noticed how very young she was.

"I've been hoping you'd ask me for a date," she said, making no attempt to conceal her liking for me.

I sat there and let the acquiescence in her eyes and the invitation in her voice start rekindling the fire. The wine slowly added fuel to the flame.

We ate mostly in silence. I ordered another bottle of wine to go, paid the waiter and once again we were out in the bitter cold night.

"Do you have to ride a bus to work?" she asked.

"No. I hated riding them. I moved to a hotel near the theatre. Now I can walk to work and back."

"I still have to take a bus."

Crossing the street, we went toward the square where the buses were stationed, but we both knew she would continue on past the square and come to my room with me.

When we had shed the heavy outer coats, I poured a little of the wine into two glasses from the bathroom. She took a sip and set her glass on the night stand.

"Don't you like the wine?"

"Yes . . . but let's first get comfortable." She turned her back, held up her hair and said, "Would you unbutton this blouse for me . . . please?"

There was nothing underneath it.

Turning back to face me, she shrugged her shoulders and let the blouse slide downwards, off the firm young breasts.

Her body had the perfection of Aphrodite—the goddess who immortalized promiscuous love.

The pants took a bit longer. She pushed them down around her knees, sat on the bed, leaned back and held up her legs for me to take them off. While I stood there with them in my hands, she began undressing me.

Lying back against the heaped up pillows, watching her settle herself on the bed, started exhilaration flowing through me like a hot current.

She sat with her knees high—the black curling hair accentuating the place where her thighs met.

I closed my eyes and imagined Jade sitting there.

Reality crowded out imagination.

Like a graceful water animal, Anina changed her position and came crawling up the bed.

Draped over me, the rhythm of her body begged for invasion.

She had obviously kissed a lot in her young life. Her lips and tongue were exciting and intent. She made flawless love. Expertly sensuous. Her thighs rose to meet each thrust, but underneath the sexual skill there was no burning flame of desire.

With me, it was purely the physical gratification of the primeval urge. When it was over there was no afterglow.

The weather was so bad, I had to ask her to stay.

"I can't. I've never stayed out all night. My mother always waits up for me."

I was glad she refused. I called a cab, gave her money for the fare.

The bottle of wine was still on the night stand, practically untouched. When I tried to read, Jade's face kept coming between my eyes and the page. I turned off the light and lay in the dark sipping the wine and watching the lights flash on and off in the beer sign across the street.

The taunting image refused to go away.

I wanted her so desperately I ached. When I could no longer control the desire, I gave myself up to the fiery tongues of passion that were licking at my groins.

Gulping the rest of the wine, I swiped at the perspiration that bathed my face. Tonight I had learned an age-old truth. When the white-hot desire for one woman is gnawing at a man's belly—no other woman's love-making can ever satisfy that desire!

Daylight was breaking when I finally got to sleep.

I awoke with the sour taste of stale wine in my mouth, and the memory of a woman I hadn't wanted in my mind, plus a monstrous headache and a nauseous stomach.

The clock showed ten o'clock. Too early to get up. My circadian rhythm hadn't yet adjusted to the rhythm of the night people.

Brushing my teeth and shaving was a losing battle. My face had so many nicks I had to open the window and scoop up a handful of snow to stop the bleeding.

I was afraid to attempt breakfast.

On the way to the theatre, a display in the window of a flower shop caught my eye. Small golden pedestals in varying heights held amber vases with yellow roses in each one.

Once I heard Jade say she loved yellow roses.

On an insane impulse, I went inside and told the wizened little man I wanted the vase with the six yellow roses.

"You'll have to carry them straight up—the stuff in the vase has a lot of moisture in it," he cautioned me. He put his artistry in a waxed box and wrapped it in many folds of thick paper. "So they won't freeze." he explained.

Walking along the street carrying a beribboned purple box, upright in my hand, I told myself I surely looked the fool that I was. I'd look a bigger fool standing at her door, like Royal Rydeen, waiting to present them.

Perhaps my sense finally cleared from the wine-fogged fantasies of last night, or maybe the cold light of day put things back in their proper perspective. Whichever, I was thankful for the return of my sanity.

I dropped the roses in the next trash bin.

CHAPTER SIXTEEN

Papa Clark had the bar cinched down. I pulled the heavy door open, and hesitated, wondering if my stomach would tolerate a cup of coffee.

Marc was sitting at the big table with his coffee in front of him and a far away look in his eyes. Dickie came in and went to the coffee niche. Without turning his head or losing his engrossed stare, Marc said, "You know you're not allowed to have coffee."

"I'm 'llowed to have tea," Dickie informed him.

Deciding to test the coffee in private, I filled a cup and started for my dressing room.

Marc came out of his trance. "Tony, would you sit down for a minute? I've been thinking about a new number."

"Oh, I thought you wuz outta town," said Dickie.

"I was. I was in Paris." Marc took a sip of his coffee and smoothed his moustache with a highly manicured fingertip. "I was in the Moulin Rouge—putting on a fabulous new Parisienne number."

"Could I be in your fab'lus new number?" Dickie extended his pinkie, took a dainty sip and smoothed an imaginary moustache with a stubby forefinger. "I could be Tom Loms A'treck."

"Shut up, Dickie!"

"Tony, I know you've never done any comedy," Marc said sounding dubious. "But learning to handle a touch of light comedy is a big asset toward getting ahead in this business."

"I don't want to get ahead in this business."

He canted his head back and stared up at me through the bottom of his glasses as though he had just encountered a new type of idiot.

"Then what in the bloody hell are you doing here?" he said. "People seldom get a job in show business to learn how to dig ditches!"

"If you remember, I did tell you I wanted to leave as soon as the police would let me go."

He lifted his eyes and seemed on the verge of taking off heavenward. When he breathed a heavy, "Jesus H. Christ!" I couldn't tell if he was searing or praying.

"The H. stands for Herkermer," exclaimed Dickie. "Jeez Herkermer Chris'."

"Why are you so upset, Marc. What's the matter?"

"Matter? Why nothing's the matter." The words dripped sarcasm. "Except as soon as those two dumb cops stop horse-assing around and get this over with, I'll have to, break in another half-assed amateur!"

"Well, there doesn't seem to be any big hurry." I said. "It'll probably be a while before they find the murderer."

He brightened like a flood light.

"Yeah, that's so," he agreed. "Personally, I don't think they could find their ass with both hands."

A strange feeling of elation coursed through me. Could it be that subconsciously I really didn't want to leave? Had Slim been right, after all?

"In that case, I'll have to do the your big Parisienne number for you, won't I?"

"Of course you will!" He sounded like Wellington at Waterloo. Then he added a bonus.

"You'll be doing the number with Tracy. She's very good doing light comedy. In fact, she's one of the best. She can carry you until you get the hang of it."

"In 'at case, she'll prolly be carryin' him on and off for the rest of her life."

"Shut up, Dickie."

Darlene came through the door and hurried to the coffee urn. Without her make-up, her face looked like a plucked chicken.

"Ye gods!" she protested hoarsely. "It's the middle of the night." The Old Taylor she had consumed last night had left her voice with a sound that was excellent for scaring crows. She took a gulp from her cup and sat down beside me.

Luttie came in, filled a cup and took a doughnut. She made the mistake of sitting beside Dickie. She drank her coffee with her elbow sticking straight out. After she'd jostled his cup a couple of times, he snarled, "Jeez Chris' Are you eatin' or tryn' to learn to fly?"

She threw her doughnut on his plate. "Here, you eat it, you little monster."

He threw it back at her. "I don' want it. Give it to the peckerwoods!"

Luttie took her cup and left. For some inexplicable reason she hadn't even given me one sex-laden glance.

Darlene stood up. "Guess I'd better go and put on my stage personality."

Dickie surveyed her blank face. "It's gonna take two layers of Kemtone this morning."

"Drop dead."

"No. Then I'd look jus' like you."

He gave me a critical once-over. "Boy, you better put on three layers an' a lot of rouge—you look like a dead fish."

He laughed. "In fact, you look like a dead fish th' cats have been fighin' over."

His jibes gave me an unpleasant jolt. I'd forgotten the nicks on my face.

Anina came through the door, and for one awful instant I was sure everybody in the room would know I'd had her in my bed last night. The nicks on my face felt like the scarlet letter.

When she merely said a pleasant "good morning" to the room, filled her cup and left, I started breathing again.

Darlene frowned. "What's the matter, Tony? Don't you feel well?"

"I feel fine. Why?"

"You're shaking like the martyr just before they put the torch to the stake."

"You musta had a real bum night," taunted Dickie.

"You've got too much mouth!"

"An' you got one helluva a hangover." He was in his glory.

"You're pretty smart, aren't you?"

"Nah," he yawned with heavy ennui. "It jus' seems that way to people who ain't smart enough."

At least I was smart enough not to go on trading insults with a six-year-old comic.

"Don't worry about the number, Marc. I'll do it. Tell Tracy to give me a lot of rehearsing." I picked up my cup and followed Darlene toward the archway. Dickie shouted after me, "I hope you throw up all over the stage!"

Quite a bit later there was the 'shave and a hair-cut' rap on the door and Tracy came in without waiting for an answer.

"What if I were undressing?" I was annoyed.

She shrugged. "You'd be undressing."

She held out a can of tomato juice. "I hear this is good for a hangover."

"Beware of the Greeks bearing gifts."

She gazed at my reflection in the mirror. "You've got too much white greasepaint under your eyes. A little will hide the dark circles—too much makes you look like a hooty owl."

I wiped away most of the excess and blended in the rest.

"That's better. Now put on some rouge. You look a bit peaked this morning."

"Did you want something or did you come in to teach me the art of make-up?"

"No. I came in to teach you the art of being a performer." She handed me some slips with lyrics on them and some with dialogue on them. "When you've finished blotting out the effects of last night's overindulgence, we can go down stairs to the piano and I'll give you your first lesson in the art of dancing—a la Gene Kelly."

"I can't dance."

"You can't read lines, either. So, I'll have to teach you how to do both, won't I?"

"Why do you have to teach me all this?" I asked cynically.

"Because Marc said he'd fire me if I didn't."

"Sorry, Trace. I guess I'm not very nice this morning."

"That's nothing new," she said with arsenic-laced sweetness. "You're never very nice at any time."

Her jibe surprised me. I'd always thought I was a very nice person.

"How did you get that impression?"

"You're so damned self-important that you remind me of the rooster who thought the sun came up every morning just to hear him crow."

"Thank you!"

"You're welcome."

"Let's go to the basement," she said. "We've got enough time before the curtain."

When we walked through the archway, Barry and Bryce were standing at the pin rail. Luttie came across the stage and went spraddle-legging up the stairs. Bryce gazed after her and said, "That Luttie sure has got a sexy little ass. I'll bet there's some might good banging there!"

"Sure is," agreed Barry. "But, sometimes it's hard to keep your mind on your business—she likes to crack jokes even when she's getting banged."

Tracy prodded my arm. "Well, do you want to learn the art of stage comedy, or do you want to learn the art of Luttie's screwing comedy?"

"Well, I'm not deaf! I couldn't help overhearing them!"

"Skip it. I was trying to be funny."

The piano in the basement was a relic with some of the ivories missing.

"We'll have to wait until Ponti comes in," she said.

"That won't be necessary." I sat down on the bench and played the Sabre Dance—just to limber up my fingers.

Her face went blank with amazement.

"What's the matter?" I smirked. "Can't you think of anything nasty to say?"

"Well, at least you can sing . . . and play the piano. Now all you have to learn is how to dance . . . and read lines . . . and acquire a little stage presence." She shrugged. "Shouldn't take you more than four or five years."

"That long, huh?"

"It'll take you that long to learn how to get out of your own way."

"Will all this make me a super actor?"

"No. You might hone the art of acting to a fine edge, but you'll never be an actor. Actors are born—not cultivated. Every actor is born under their own lucky star. It gives them magic. It shines on them as long as they live—it guides their career."

"Then I'll get me a lucky star."

"A sky full of lucky stars wouldn't help you!"

"Do you believe in the Tooth Fairy and Santa Claus?"

"No. But I do believe that all the half-assed ancestor-worshipping, chicken-shit snobs are hatched in New England! From rotten eggs!"

BOOK FIVE

Jade LeMare

Show business is a game of roulette
We actors are the little bouncing balls
Fate spins the wheel
Sometimes we win
Sometimes we lose

"Irish"

CHAPTER SEVENTEEN

More than two weeks had passed since Aidey's murder and the police still had nothing tangible to go on. The reporters had ceased camping around the stage door and gone on to more recent murders. The newspapers had relegated our murder to the section reserved for the "Orbits" and "Your Horoscope."

Mulchahe and O'Brien still came around everyday. Sometimes accompanied by one or two uniformed officers, who were more interested in standing in the wings watching the show than in murder. Especially the younger ones who hadn't forgotten how to laugh.

A new girl had been hired to take Aidey's place. Luttie spent a lot of time backstage—invariably doing her seesawing grind while she brazenly gave each new young officer the come-on. Clearly she considered herself a prime contender for a gold medal in the Sex Olympics.

Today a most handsome officer had shown up. He was tall with wavy blond hair and a devastating dimple in his chin. Luttie had him cornered in the second wing. While she seesawed, she was sliding upward glances at him with ponderous attempts at being seductive.

She was getting across about like an elephant on a trapeze.

There were too many beautiful young girls flitting about with some of the bobblingest bosoms that ever bedeviled a man's baser instincts, for him to waste time on a flabby-titted old frog who was staving off forty.

He began ignoring her so pointedly she gave up and headed for Barry's office. She was sure of a score there.

As she cantered past the switchboard, Mulchahe said, "That little broad hustles fast, don't she?"

"Yeah," said Slim. "She'll trip you and be under you before you hit the floor."

I had lingered by the switchboard to see if I could hear any new details. If Mulchahe knew any, he was keeping them to himself.

Tony went by with barely a nod for the three of us. I smiled with smug satisfaction as I went to my room. I had the gentleman checkmated. He couldn't leave the company and he couldn't refuse to do the Anthony and Cleopatra number. All he could do was sit on the stage, in a burlesque theatre, while a near-naked female writhed over him like a succuba raping a captive male. I knew I had more than evened the score for the brush-off in the hotel lobby.

Dickie kicked on the door. "Can I come in, Jade?"

"No. I'm busy."

"You are not. . .Jade . . .I have to tell you somethin'."

All right, come on in, you little pest."

He eased through the door and climbed silently into my old guest chair. Could this be Dickie? Not the one I knew. He had a telltale glistening in his eyes and the pugnacious chin was definitely quivering.

"What's wrong? Why are you crying?"

"I'm not crying," he denied manfully. A big tear slid from the corner of his eye and down his face. He put out his tongue and licked it away.

"Why are you crying?" I asked again.

"Cause . . . I . . . well, I wuz playin' with that little car Aidey gave me. An' I started thinkin' about her gettin' hurt." His voice caught on a sob. "I felt awful sorry, cause Aidey got hurt."

I'm sorry too."

"You didn't like her, did you?"

"No, I didn't like her, but I never wanted her to get hurt."

"Aidey wuz good to me. She didn't shove me and push me like the rest of these son-a-bitchin' people do. One night that mean ol' Royal shoved me out of his way so hard my head hit the radiator. Aidey wuz sittin' on the bench . . . an' she rubbed my head and helped me not to cry."

"That showed Aidey liked you a lot."

"I know it."

He was quiet for so long that I said, "Was that what you wanted to tell me?"

"Well . . . yes . . . kinda. You know that real pretty stage money I gived you?"

"Yes." I laid aside the crossword puzzle and waited. He sometimes went by way of Paducah to get to the point.

"Well . . . I . . . had two pieces."

"You did?" I tried to hide my surprise.

"I hid it in my teddy bear, behind that thing that squeaks. Well . . . the night Aidey helped me not to cry, I took it out and gived it to her."

"Do you remember which night you gave it to her?"

"It wuz the night Luttie had that party for Barry."

"Was she surprised at how pretty it was?"

"Nah, it wuz dark there by the radiator. She didn't look at it good. She put it in her pocket and said, someday she wuz gonna have a little boy like me and he could play with it."

My mind started doing some bizarre speculating. Dickie had given Aidey the coin—and she had been murdered that same night.

Could it be? No. Never.

It was inconceivable to think anyone would commit murder for a twenty dollar gold piece.

"I wonder what she did with her coat that night. She didn't go home. Your stage money must still be in the pocket."

"No, it ain't."

"How do you know?"

"Cause her coat is hanging in the prop room. When I saw it there . . . well . . . I put my hand in the pocket to see if the money wuz still there. Aidey couldn't never have it no more, an' I wanted it back." He slid out of the chair. "Maybe it's on the floor. I'll go look for it."

"Dickie, you know you were told to stay out of the prop room," I said. "So don't you go back in there."

"All right, I won't," he said slamming the door.

And I sat there wondering if I should tell Mulchahe about the coat and the gold coin. I decided to keep quiet. Besides, I wanted to think about where Dickie could have gotten those coins. It wasn't likely somebody could have lost two of them in the same place.

Then something started playing hide and seek in my head. I closed my eyes and tried to dredge up the illusive memory that hovered just above my thoughts.

Ah, old Ned.

That first day when I went to the basement, he had told me there was no use looking for it down there. What had he thought I was looking for? Did he believe there was something hidden somewhere in this old theatre?

Maybe something like a cache of gold coins?

Trying to pump him would be as futile as trying to pump ice water from the Phlegethon. So I settled for Slim. He'd been here for years. Maybe he might know what Old Ned had been hinting about.

I took a pillow as protection against the iron stool and went to visit Slim. After some idle speculation about whether the police had any clues they weren't revealing, I asked, "How long have you been working here, Slim?"

"Well . . . let's see . . .on and off. . .about forty years." He shook his head in disbelief. "It sure doesn't seem that long."

"That's the glory of our world, Slim. When you're living in Never-Never Land, you don't hear the ticking of the clock."

"Old Jerome Rosen had five other theatres. I worked in all of them, but I liked this one best. I met my wife here when it opened. She was the first cashier."

"What was old man Rosen like? Your wife must've known him pretty well back then."

"Nobody knew him pretty well at any time. He was a dried up old miser—eccentric as hell and twice as stingy. I never saw anyone that liked him. He was close-mouthed and unfriendly and as hateful as he could be. This theatre was his headquarters. He used to stay here two or three times a week. He'd sleep on that big leather divan up there in his office."

"My! What a charming old gentleman. Who ran the theatres after he died?"

"His wife tried to, she knew nothing about show business, or managing a theatre. After a couple of years, she started to sell them off, one at a time, as she needed the money. She hung onto this one until the last. . ."

"Why would she have to sell the theatres? He must've been a millionaire."

"That's what everybody thought, until she hired an attorney and started going through his books and records. The only assets he left were the theatres."

"Six theatres had to take in an awful lot of money. Maybe the old guy didn't trust banks. Maybe he stashed all his money away somewhere."

Slim laughed his dry laugh. "I wondered why you were asking all those questions." He eyed me with a puzzled frown. "I thought those old rumors had been forgotten years ago. Who told you about them?"

Nobody. But the first day I was here I went down to the basement to see about some heat. Old Ned was very hostile. He seemed to think I was down there looking for something. He told me I wouldn't find it down there."

"Ned was working here when old man Rosen died. I guess he thinks the old man hid a fortune somewhere in this theatre."

"Maybe he's right. Did anybody ever try to find it?"

"His wife. Since this was his headquarters, she figured if there was any money hidden anywhere it would be here. She hired a couple of guys and for weeks they went over the place with a fine toothed comb, but they never found anything."

"Maybe he had an expensive mistress."

"That rumor went around, too. Nobody ever found out who she was—if there was one."

"Well then, maybe he had two or three mistresses and a mania for gambling. Fast women and slow horses have kept a lot of men broke."

Tracy came out for the last scene and reminded me it was almost time for my number.

While I dressed, I let my titanic imagination crystallize into a wild idea. All those intriguing old rumors made me think my idea just might have some substance.

At intermission I asked Tramp and Arlete if Dickie could have dinner with me. Since this was one of his greatest treats, he was delighted.

As soon as the finale was over, he appeared carrying his overcoat and galoshes. His hands and face were scrubbed and for once his hair was combed. "C'mon, les go," he urged.

"Okay. But at least give me time to get dressed."

"Oh, I forgot somethin'." He piled his things on the day bed and darted back out the door. When he returned, his pants were threatening to slip their moorings.

"Sorry chum, but you can't take that magnet with you."

"Aw Jeez Chris', I can't never do nothin'. Why can't I take it with me?"

"Because the waiter might not like it when you start making trains out of the silverware."

He dragged it out of his pocket and before I could stop him he chug-chugged it across the dressing shelf, picking up a nail file, scissors, tweezers, etc.

"Will you put that thing away!" Everything on my shelf is magnetized now!"

"Aw rats." He put the magnet under the pillow on the bed.

"You're a pest. Go sit outside until I get dressed."

I stalled for time. I wanted everybody else to be out by the time I finished. My emotions seesawed between leaping excitement and apprehensive dread. My vague hopes were seeded with vaguer fears.

When I opened the door, he was sitting in the chair looking like a volcano about to erupt. "What the devil took you so long? I'm starvin' to death!"

"We'll go in a minute. But first I want you to do me a small-type favor."

I held the door open for him to pass back through. He gave me a wise look as he sidled by. Dickie was only kneel-high to a gosling but he knew when he was being euchred.

"I gotta sing for my supper, huh?"

"Of course not. It's really nothing. All you have to do is show me where you found that pretty stage money."

"Jeez Chris', Jade! I jus' found 'em. I tole you I didn't 'emember where I found the damn things."

"I think you're fibbing."

The angry pout on his face looked like a thundercloud.

"Were there any more where you found those?"

"Yeah! Yeah!" he burst out angrily. "There wuz a whole bunch of 'em."

Even though I had sensed what was coming, I felt a thrill of excitement. I smiled sweetly at him.

"Okay, now we can go to dinner—as soon as you show me where you found all that pretty stage money."

"No!" he said, as his jaw set in mutinous refusal. "Ta hell with the lousy dinner . . . I didn't wanna go nohow."

"Why don't you want to show me the place, sweetie pie?"

"Cause I ain't never goin' back up there no more, that's why. It's too scary. It makes your breath all chokey . . . an' when you want to come back down, you get a funny feelin' like you're gonna fall. I almost didn't never get back down."

"Good heavens! Did you climb up to the fly loft?"

The fly loft was at least forty feet above the stage.

"Yeah."

"You damn-fool little demon, you could have broken your neck! If you'd fallen you would've been killed!" I dragged in a deep breath and exhaled some of the fright he'd given me. "What ever possessed you to go climbing up there?"

"Well . . . the rehearsal wuz on . . . an' I didn't have nothin' to do. I wuz sittin' on th' bench . . . right there beside th' ladder. Nobody wuz lookin' an I jus' started climbing."

"Okay, Daredevil Dickie, then what?"

"Well it wuz kinda dark up there on the catwalk, but I crawled over to th' front where a little bit of light shines up from the stage."

"Are you making up a big tale about finding the money up there? Stagehands have been going up there for forty years—how come none of them ever found it?"

"Honest to God, I did, Jade. They're all in a little bitty room with a whole lot of other ol' junk. Nobody found 'em cause you can't tell the little room is there. It's a secret room."

"We'll wait until we're sure everybody else is gone, then you can show me the secret place."

"No." He said with flat finality. "I ain't never gonna climb back up there no more."

"I'm surprised at you. I thought you were never afraid."

"I ain't afraid. It's jus' all them funny feelin's when you're up so high . . . like you can't keep from fallin'."

"I'll help you," I reassured him. Which was like offering a rubber crutch to Tiny Tim. I'm scared witless of height.

"For Chris' sake, why'da want to climb all the way up there jus' to look at a bunch of ol' slugs?"

"Because they're so pretty. I want to send one to my kid sister." (I didn't have a kid sister, but he didn't know that.) "She can wear it on a chain. That's what I'm going to do with mine—wear it on a gold chain around my neck."

"Can I get one for Arlete?"

"Of course."

He glowered for a moment. "All right, but I have to take my magnet with me."

I was so elated, I'd have agreed to let him drag his old tricycle up the ladder.

When the coast was clear, I closed the door and locked the padlock, then pinned the key to the waistband of my slacks.

He climbed up two rungs ahead of me. I stepped up on the bottom rung with my hands grasping the rungs on either side of his feet. "See, I've got you locked in. You couldn't fall if you wanted to."

When we reached the top I was gasping for breath. My knees felt like I'd done a ten chorus tiller routine. Even Dickie was puffing. We sat on the catwalk while I refilled my lungs.

"Are you afraid, Jade?" whispered Dickie.

"Well, let's just say I don't ever want a job as a flyman."

"No use standing up," he pointed out sensibly. "We can crawl over to the front."

At the front, I peered down at the stage. It looked a mile below us. Dickie stood up and moved a step toward the front wall. He ran his hand over to a small slidebolt. He pulled it back and pushed open a half-sized door.

"Well . . . are ya gonna sit there all day?"

With the aid of the railing, I got to my feet, bent down and followed him through the door.

When the Empress was built, a Grand Wurlitzer organ had been installed. The huge organ was long since gone, but the old sound chambers had been left intact. Dickie twisted a light button inside the door and I discovered we were inside one of the chambers.

"No one has been in here for years and years, and the light still burns," I marvelled.

"That's cause it ain't never been burned none in years and years."

"Little smarty pants."

Our voices echoed off the walls with a hollow, sepulchral sound. Half a century of dust and cobwebs gave things the eerie look of a movie scene in a haunted tower. All my saner instincts told me to get the hell out.

Pipes of all shapes and sizes sprouted up through the floor. Others were set in wooden tiers around the circular walls. Some flared at the tops, but most of them looked like they belonged on a steam calliope. In the thick dust on the floor, a trail of small footprints could be seen in and out through the forest of pipes.

The walls were lined with squares—probably for acoustical reasons. At the front was an open iron grid camouflaged from the audience by a lot of flaking della robia and grimy cherubim. There wasn't a place where a small mouse could have hidden.

"All right, Short John Silver, where's the treasure chest?"

"Step right this way, folks." He took out his magnet and began spieling. "Abra-ca-dab-ra . . . bits-bab-a-loo . . . ass-bas-billy us . . . spit in your shoe."

"Will you stop hamming it up?"

"Geez, you're a lousy audience—case ya don't know it."

He crossed the floor and put his magnet against the wall and began sliding it along in a weaving path. "Step right up, folks. . ."

"Dickie!"

When the pint-sized prestidigitator felt the magnet catch, he paused dramatically, gave a tug and one of the wooden squares swung out to reveal a black hole beyond.

My jaw went slack as I stared. Then I thought how ingenious, but how utterly simple. An iron disc was imbedded in the back side of the panel. When a strong magnet was held against the front, over the disk, the panel swung open easily.

I slid the magnet off the panel and said, "Dickie, how in all heaven and hell did you ever manage to find that one little spot? The odds are about ten million to one!"

"Well . . . I wuz walkin' around puttin' my magnet on all them pipes . . . it stuck real hard on 'em. Then I started pushin' it along the wall playin' train. When it got here it stuck. I pulled real hard . . . an' PRESTO!" He gave me a smug grin.

"Can you presto a light inside that hole?"

"Sure." He reached inside and twisted a button and a feeble light sprang to life.

"Ya gotta be an actorbat to get through this little hole."

The hole was like a small window. It was about two feet above the floor. To get through the narrow opening, you had to put one leg in first, bend double and ease yourself across the sill. Dickie's legs were a little short for the feat, but he managed.

My heart was leaping like a drunken kangaroo as I put my leg through the hole and squeezed the rest of me in after him.

CHAPTER EIGHTEEN

There was barely head room as I stood up to look around the small retreat. What had been a dead space between the curve of the organ chamber and the proscenium wall had been converted into a miser's secret vault.

An elegant gold opera chair sat in front of four stacked boxes that had obviously served as a desk. Alongside the make-shift desk, two more boxes supported a thick piece of board. Stacked on the board were about fifty old cigar boxes.

Dickie lifted the lid on one of them in the top row.

"See, there's a whole bunch of that pretty money in 'ese boxes."

Staring down at the contents of that cigar box sent my senses reeling. With unsteady fingers I removed one stack of the coins and counted them. Then I counted the rows and used my fingers to multiply. There was six thousand dollars in that box! If all those boxes were full, there was about half a million dollars in gold stashed in that little room. The thought made my ears roar.

Putting the stack back into the box, I examined the dates on each one before letting it clink back in place. All of them were dated between fifty and sixty years earlier. The United States had been off the gold standard for a long time. That meant those coins were worth a lot more than their face value.

"Jade, are you deaf? Why'nt ya answer me when I talk to you?"

"Sorry sweetie, I was thinking about something else. What did you say?"

"I ast you if I could take two of 'em to keep for the ones I gived you and Aidey."

Aidey? Aidey had one of the gold pieces! What if my first vague suspicions about a link between the gold piece and murder wasn't so farfetched after all? I felt a tingle of apprehension zigzag up my spine.

"Let's get out of here now," I said. "This place gives me the creeps."

"You didn't say if I could take 'em or not. I ain't never comin' back here no more. I wanna take 'em with me now!"

"All right. But you'll have to let me keep them for you."

"Why do you hafta keep 'em?"

"I'll explain later." I handed him two double eagles and dropped one in each of my shoes. Then Satan looked over my shoulder and cooed, "Two isn't enough. Why don't you take two more?" So I dropped two more in my shoes. Then two more for good luck.

"Okay, let's go," I said, pausing to look around the little room. I'd been so engrossed in that gold, I hadn't noticed anything else.

Piled against the back wall were six huge leatherbound ledgers. I raised the cover of one and saw, RIALTO THE-ATRE, over a column of tightly written figures. The next one was for the MAYFAIR THEATRE, and the next for the BIJOU THEATRE. I didn't look at the other three. It was plain that they were old Jerome Rozen's authentic set of books.

On the desk were old programs, handbills, a stack of old letters, and an ornate silver inkwell with the ink dried to a crust. An enameled pen was beside the inkwell.

Tacked to the wall near the small entrance was a big poster showing a girly wearing a wasp-waisted, low cut gown and a large feathered hat. The billing proclaimed her to be, THE RAVISHINGLY BEAUTIFUL GABY LEGERE. THE DARLING OF TWO CONTINENTS. Under the heavy film of dust, she looked strangely familiar.

Below the poster, a small pedestal held something covered by a piece of faded velour. I removed the velour and caught my breath in delight. There sat a fabulous hand-painted porcelain jewel chest. It was in a gold ormolu footed frame with an ornate gold handle across the lid.

Inside was a folded handkerchief, a gold hairpin and one long white silk glove. Here was a shrine to an old man's beloved mistress.

I stepped back and studied the poster, puzzled by the familiar look. Her head was tilted in a flirtatious pose. One slim hand was on her hip and the other rested on the handle of a beaded parasol.

Using the clean side of the velour, I wiped the dust from the beautiful face, and frowned at the likeness.

Gaby Legere had surely been reincarnated. She was now Caralyn Ayeres!

"Gee, Jade, how did Caralyn's picture get up here? That sure is a pretty costume."

"That couldn't be Caralyn's picture. That picture was made . . . probably fifty years ago. That girl may be dead by now."

"How comes she looks so much like Caralyn?"

"Coincidence, I guess."

I started to put the velour back on the little chest, but hesitated when Dickie's voice echoed my own thoughts.

"Jade, let's take that pretty box and give it to Caralyn."

Only I hadn't exactly planned on giving it to Caralyn.

"Why do you want to give it to her?"

"Cause she looks so much like that girl it belonged to."

"Why do you think it belonged to the girl in the picture?"

"Well . . . somebody put it there under her picture, an' the things in it must a been her things. If she's dead, she can't have it no more. Let's give it to Caralyn."

"We can't. There's no way I could climb back down the ladder with it. I need both hands to hold onto the ladder."

"You could carry it if ya put it up your pant's leg an' nen tied your scarf under it real tight. That way it couldn't fall."

"If I live to be a hundred, maybe somewhere along the way I'll learn to think as fast as you do, my little genius."

We turned the light out, squeezed back through the hole and closed the wooden square. There was no way anybody could tell it was different from the others.

While exiting the organ chamber, we slipped the bolt back into place and climbed back down the ladder. All the way down, I had a nightmarish fear that I would fall before I reached the bottom.

Despite his arguments I locked his coins along with mine, and the box, in my trunk. Then we brushed our clothes, washed our hands and got into our coats. It felt like time had run backwards for fifty years.

As a reward, I let him pick the restaurant. He picked an expensive steak house, then ordered a ham'ugger samitch.

While we waited, I noticed he kept glowering down at the table with his under-lip thrust out in a pout.

"What are you pouting about?"

"I wanted to keep my own money. I wanted to give it to Arlete."

"You can't. You can't even let her know you have them."

"Why can't I?"

I tried to fabricate a plausible story to tell him, then decided to tell him the truth.

"Because that isn't stage money. All the money up there is real money—solid gold money."

"I know it."

All I could do was stare at him.

"At first I thought it was play money, then I knowed it was real."

"How did you find out it was real?"

"Well . . . when you saw that boxful . . . you looked like a comic doin' a double-take . . . when you got through countin' on your fingers you looked punch drunk as hell. Nen you started rubbin' 'em and lookin' at 'em real close. Nobody'd be doin' all that countin' and 'zaminin' on a bunch of old stage money."

And I thought he'd believe any story I cooked up. Ha! I should live so long.

"Jade, who hid all that money up there?"

"The old man who built this theatre a long time ago."

"What'd he hide it for?"

"Everybody says he was a tight-fisted old miser. So, he must've hid it up there because he didn't want anyone to know he had all that gold. He died without ever telling anybody anything about it."

"Well . . . if he's dead . . . who belongs to the money?"

"His wife, if she's still living. She might have some kind of claim. Otherwise, I suppose it would belong to Herlick and Nathan. Since they own the theatre."

"In that case, we shoulda took a whole boxful."

"No we shouldn't", I said sternly. "That would be steal-ing!"

Filling your shoes with souvenirs wasn't stealing.

"If anybody else knowed it waits up there, they'd be stealin' it, wouldn't they?"

"You can bet your sweet ankle they would!"

"It ain't sweet ankle."

"Dickie, we have to be real careful. I'm sure somebody believes there's a lot of money hidden in this old theatre. If they knew we found it, they might do something terrible to us to make us tell them where it's hidden. That's the reason we have to keep it a secret. I want you to promise you won't say one word to anybody about it."

He held up a stubby hand. "I promise I won't say nothin' to nobody."

He saw the waiter approaching and promptly lost interest in such trifling things as boxes of gold money.

"Jeez Chris', where've ya been? I'm starvin' to death. I hope ya put lots of ung'yons on my samitch . . . an' I want some ketchup an' some mustard an pickles an a choc'lit malted milk."

"Isn't it about time you learned how to say please?"

"I know how," he dead-panned.

When we finished dinner, we went to my hotel and I made him lie down for a nap.

"Aw, why do I haf'ta take a nap? I ain't no baby."

"I promised your mother you'd take a nap, that's why."

Exhausted by the incredible events of the last two hours, I settled down beside him and tried to think of answers to some very pertinent questions—like what to do about a half million dollars in gold? And how many people might know about those old rumors? How many might believe they were true? Who would be the most likely to suspect that Aidey's coin might have come from a hidden cache?

I had the choice of revealing where it was hidden and maybe finding myself a prime suspect in a murder—or keeping quiet and, perhaps, becoming the next victim.

Even though I told myself I was letting my imagination run away with my alleged common sense, I made a mental vow not to voice any of those questions out loud.

CHAPTER NINETEEN

The opening was on when we arrived at the theatre, so we had to go around behind the backdrop. As we passed the doorway to the wardrobe room, I stumbled over Penny.

"For heaven's sake, Penny, will you get up off the floor. Can't you hear? The opening is on."

My eyes hadn't adjusted from the bright snow to the dim reflection behind the curtain. But as I squinted down, I saw instantly that it wasn't Penny there on the floor. For one awful moment I thought I was going to faint.

Then I was on my knees tearing frantically at the length of the trickline that was knotted tightly around Caralyn Ayres' lovely white throat.

I shoved at Dickie. "Go tell Slim. Tell him to call an ambulance!"

When I couldn't unloosen the knot, I began screaming for Barry. In seconds he came running from the switchboard side.

"It's Caralyn, I think she's dead! I can't get the rope loose. Hurry, please hurry and get it loose."

He loosened the knot instantly. He was trying to say something, but his words were incoherent with shock.

"Can't you help her?" I pleaded.

He shook his head.

Huey seemed to materialize out of thin air, demanding to know, "Who in the hell is doing all that stupid screaming?" Then he looked down and gasped, "Oh my God! On no, not Caralyn!"

I was conscious of people crowding close to see what had happened, smothering gasps of horror when they saw it was Caralyn.

"Tony knelt beside Barry and said, "Let me take over."

"It's no use . . . you can't help her."

The scene was taking on the slow-motion futility of trying to outrun the lions in a nightmare. Bryce Reagan was vainly trying to get people away to do the scenes or numbers. Slim yelled, "Where in the hell is that damned ambulance? They've got oxygen tanks on them."

"It's too late for oxygen." said Chou Chou.

Two men appeared from O.P. making a commotion at they tried to maneuver a gurney through the clutter behind the curtain.

Dickie tugged at my hand, "Jade . . . is Carlyn hurt real bad . . . like Aidey wuz?"

"Yes, I think she is."

He held my hand and said, "Let's go sit in your room."

Barry was standing in the hall with a look of stunned disbelief on his face. "Maybe if I had known . . . what to do . . ."

"Nobody knew what to do. Maybe if I could've got that knot loose quicker."

"It was a clove hitch," he said woodenly.

"Yes, I know. I just couldn't get it loose."

"Somebody here is a psycho—there's no sane reason why anyone would murder her."

Tracy and Darlene were coming down the stairs. They turned the landing in time to hear my remark.

"Why don't you stop playing detective, Jade." Tracy said with some exasperation. "You make a better strip woman than a gumshoe."

I was on the verge of making a defensive retort, then I realized she thought I was rehashing Aidey's murder. It's incredible I thought, but half of the people backstage aren't yet aware that we'll have to live through another murder.

"You tell them, Barry," I said as I pushed Dickie into my dressing room and closed the door.

He watched my shaking hands as I tried to redo my make-up.

"Don't be nervous—you'll stink up your number."

"Why don't they just bring down the curtain?" I said. "When everybody finds out, the show will be a disaster. Nobody can go out on stage and act natural."

"Jade . . . why would anybody want to hurt Caralyn?"

"I don't know. I don't know anything about her. I don't even know why she was here."

"She works here," he said, frowning at my stupidity.

To Dickie, Caralyn wasn't a princess masquerading as a peasant. She was just the singer who worked in the show.

But to me, she was still an enigma. Everything about her spelled top drawer. Her gowns were Paris. Her jewelry Cartier. Which added up to the rigid total that two hundred dollars a week would be peanuts to her. So, why was she working here? There had to be some logical reason.

That's when the light went on over my head.

Could the reason be that she knew something about a fortune in gold? Could it be that her striking resemblance to the girl on the poster was not a coincidence? She was too young to be Gaby Legere's daughter, but the right age to be her granddaughter. If Gaby Legere had been old Jerome Rozen's mistress, then she could have told Caralyn about the gold the old miser had stashed somewhere in this theatre.

Finding that roomful of gold had started my brain on a merry-go-round of questions. Finding Caralyn's body had suddenly given those questions some very plausible answers. Answers that made my heart start acting like a broken pump.

I put on my Cleopatra costume and stared into the mirror. Cleopatra stared back as though she had just discovered her barge was sinking.

Tracy came in, gave me a long worried look and said, "You look like you're going to faint."

"I feel like it, too." I stood up and she sank limply into my chair.

"Do you really think Barry is capable of murdering anyone?" she asked.

"I don't know, but I'm almost sure he had nothing to do with Caralyn's murder."

"Why?"

"He was absolutely stunned when he saw her there with that rope around her neck."

"Could he have been faking?"

"No, he's not that good an actor."

"Then who?"

"That's the big question. And 'why' is a bigger one."

She stood up. "I'll go get Arlete's smelling salts— you need a sniff."

I gave one last critical glance in the mirror. A grimace to see if the teeth was free of lipstick. A push-pull at the hair, and Cleo went out to board her sinking barge.

She met me in the hall and I sniffed the stuff in the bottle. When the top of my head settled back in place, we went out on stage.

It was easy to see the news had travelled through the cast like shock waves. Different faces reflected different reactions, but all mirrored the same baffling fear.

Tony was sitting in the Roman seat waiting to sing my trailers. As he adjusted the mike and tightened the set screw, I noticed how strong his hands looked. Where they capable of jerking a deadly clove hitch tight around a throat? Did he know who Caralyn was? Did he know why she was here? She had talked to him more than anyone else. I turned away and tried to thrust such macabre thoughts from my mind.

Slim had his hand on the master switch, waiting to pull the blackout. Tramp and Arlete were on the other side waiting for the finale. There would be no one in their dressing room.

"Dickie, you stand here by the stools and wait until I finish my number." For some inexplicable reason I was unwilling to send him to his room, where he would be alone.

"I can't. You know they'll chase me."

"Maybe not. I doubt if anyone will even notice you."

I paraded through my first trailer with my mind totally occupied with murder. At intervals, I paused to do a few pallid wiggles that could have been outdone by a consumptive worm. The audience repaid me in kind. Dickie was right. I was stinking up my number.

Back in my dressing room, I sank into my chair and prayed fervently the audience would go home before the curtain went up for the second act.

An imperative knock interrupted my prayers. Before the knock came again, I knew who was standing out there. No one except a policeman can put that much demand in a knock.

Dickie opened the door and my two granite friends came in. As before, with none of the preliminary amenities, Mulcahe began asking his intimidating questions.

"You found this one too?" He made it sound like I was the official body finder.

"Yes"

"Well go on."

I looked at him blankly.

"How did you happen to find her?"

"Dickie and I were coming around behind the backdrop and I stumbled. . . over. . her. It's rather dim back there.

"What reason would she have for going back there in the dark" he asked.

I realized all cops considered all actors to be moronic, so I decided to help him prove his theory.

"The same reason the chicken had for crossing the road—she wanted to get to the other side." I said.

Both ignored the flip answer, but two granite visages hardened up quite a bit.

"Did you see anyone else back there?"

"No."

"It wuz real dimlike back there," put in Dickie.

"We can do without your help, my little man, so scat."

"I ain't your little man!" Dickie glared at him. "An' you can go to hell!" He went out and slammed the door.

"You'll have to forgive his manners." I said. "He's usually a pretty good kid, but he had a mighty big scare and he's still rather badly shaken up."

"His manners are the same whether he's scared or not," said O'Brien. "He's a bratty little wisenheimer."

Mulchahe cleared the sharp irritation out of his throat. "You say there was no one else back there?"

"I didn't see anybody."

"Would you have noticed anyone leaving before you stumbled over the body?"

Stumbling over Caralyn's body had been a terrible shock. Now, delayed reaction was coming and going in waves. It was also affecting my ability to control my tongue.

"I'm sure I would have." I said. "I'm fairly bright —
when I was only nine years old, I could wave bye-bye." I
went over to the daybed and curled up against the pillows.
"Please go away!"

They didn't go away. They stone-eyed me into silence.

"A few more questions—if you don't mind."

"I do mind," I said. "I'd like to relax for awhile before
I have to go back out into the arena again."

"This won't take long."

"Why are you asking me all these questions? I know
absolutely nothing at all about the girl. She worked here.
Someone murdered her. That's all I know!"

"What kind of a girl was she?"

"She was a lady. Although I'm sure you couldn't possibly believe that."

"Do you know anybody who didn't like her?"

"No! Everybody liked Caralyn," I said emphatically.
Then added, "And that's strange."

"What's strange?"

"Well . . . everybody liked Caralyn, and almost nobody
liked Aidey."

His stare asked the question.

"I'm sure the same person murdered both of them."

Surprise flitted across his face. "Now what makes you
think the same person murdered them both?" The surprise
didn't keep him from being sarcastic.

"Both times he used a piece of trickline and both times
he used a clove hitch to strangle them."

"He? Why do you think it was a man? Women commit
murder too, you know."

"Yes but very few women know how to make a clove
hitch and not many of them could subdue a girl as big as
Aidey."

"What is a clove hitch?" asked O'Brien.

"It's a knot stagehands use. When it's pulled tight it
sorta locks itself."

"Looks like we'd better talk to the stagehands."

"Before you get carried away, anyone who works in a theatre can learn to form a clove hitch."

He eyed me with an arctic stab. "Can you?"

"Yes."

"You say both girls were strangled with the same kind of knot?"

Actually I had only seen the trickline around Aidey's neck, not the knot. When I found Caralyn strangled with the same kind of rope, and Barry said it was a clove hitch, I had unconsciously surmised the same kind of knot would have been in the rope around Aidey's throat. But, it was too late to start crawfishing now!

"Yes," I said, praying they'd forget all about clove hitches.

"Did you examine the knots?"

"No, of course not!"

"Then how do you know what kind they were?" His look accused me of all kinds of covert knowledge.

"I suppose I heard someone mention that they were?" I wasn't going to tell him that Barry had said the one on Caralyn's throat was one. "What difference does it make?" I asked angrily. "It's not important."

My eyes met Mulchahe's ice blue stare and I knew he was getting mighty annoyed with my snip-snap lip.

"I'll be the judge of what's important and what's not important," he said. "Now why didn't you mention all this when the first girl was murdered?"

"Because nobody ever asked me if the murderer used a clove hitch—or a half hitch—or any of the other hitches!" My voice rose to an hysterical shriek. "And if you want to know why he used that particular knot, I imagine it's be-cause he could fashion the loop, drop it over the victim's head, jerk the ends tight and then disappear. His victim would still choke to death!"

I turned my back and put the pillow over my head.

As they went out the door, O'Brien said, "That dame and that kid are a couple of smart asses."

If there is any truth in that old saw about the Guy in the sky taking care of babies and half-wits, then he should have rung a warning bell—because in the last half hour, I had definitely proven that I belonged in the latter category.

BOOK SIX

Anthony Clay Blake

The Moving Finger writes; and having writ,
Moves on; nor all your piety nor Wit
Shall lure it back to cancel half a Line,
Nor all your Tears wash out a Word of it.

Omar Khayyam

CHAPTER TWENTY

When Caralyn's murder hit the front pages, the newspapers had a Roman holiday. A second murder backstage in a burlesque theatre was more than they could ever have hoped for.

Each day the scareheads were bolder and the details gorier as they ballyhooed the news to the sensation-hungry public. And each day that same public jammed the theatre as bloodthirsty spectators. Every performance was sold out in advance to these strange fanatics.

The management took advantage of their weird curiosity by raising the price of admission, but still they came in droves.

They displayed a derisive amusement toward the comics and a yawning ennui for the strip women and the dancers. Apparently they only came to sit and speculate— loudly— which one of the actors would turn out to be the murderer.

I found myself resenting the newspaper editorials. Especially when they referred to Caralyn as just another burlesque queen.

During the hullabaloo, the city's leading paper sent one of their reporters around to interview the people backstage. Since it was the paper that carried all the advertisements and all the publicity for the theatre, the Gruesome Twosome personally escorted him back stage and gave him liberty to interview the people.

His masterpiece came out in the Sunday supplement. It was filled with hackneyed phrases about the way performers looked, talked and acted. He allocated the same basic character to all, male and female alike. Mentality, low. Morals, low. Prime interest in life, sex. Hobbies, sex. Background, low-class trash. All the women were cheap and vulgar. All the men were ignorant and uncouth.

It was written from the viewpoint of a man who knew everything about the tawdry trade of burlesque.

Yet the sum total of his vast knowledge was one day spent backstage. And the extent of his depthless research was an exhaustive inquisition into sex. His questions were designed to ferret out any aberrant sexual inclinations anyone might have. All for his own private files, no doubt.

He asked the women for their views on lesbianism and group sex. The men were asked if they could indulge in sex with all the women in the cast. He insisted these personal questions were "off the record." When he put his "off the record" questions to Slim, Slim said, "Why don't you go fuck yourself and write about that?"

Naturally, he didn't manage to collect much information. But he did manage to make a lot of trips to Barry's office to swig down the free liquor Huey had sent back for him.

I read his article over breakfast in the little deli. It infuriated me. He described me as the typical male one found in burlesque. Long on looks. Short on brains. No talent. Not enough ability to make it in legitimate show business. He made me look like a simple-minded gigolo.

Jade and Tracy were sitting on the stools, having their morning tea, when I came across the stage with the paper in my hand. Tracy indicated the paper with the doughnut she was eating.

"Have you read what an unsavory lot we are?" she asked.

Yes, and I'd like to smash his face!"

"Don't let it bother you," she shrugged. "He is merely beating the Devil. Everything he's wrote has been written by every drunken hack who ever wrote anything about burlesque."

"We've read it all dozens of times before," said Jade.

"Don't you people care when they write these degrading things about you?"

"No. Not at all," said Tracy. "We don't feel the slings and arrows of the outraged hypocrites as keenly as other people do. It isn't that our skin is thicker or our perception duller. It's just that we're used to them."

"I'd still like to break his head!"

"How strange," said Jade. "Why this sudden turnabout?"

"After Aidey's murder, you thought this kind of bilge was on a par with the Sermon On The Mount." Her green eyes regarded me with such a direct challenge, it was difficult not to shift my gaze away.

"Yeah," said Tracy. "Why are you so boiled-up, now?"

"This . . . have you read what this creep said about me?"

"Yes, we did. Seems he doesn't think much of you as an actor, or as a member of the human race, for that matter."

"He knows nothing about me. He has no right to print such things."

"You think he may have been mistaken in his opinion of you?" asked Jade. "You think he may have besmirched your good name and your character with his garbage?"

"I certainly do!"

"But after Aidey's murder, you thought their salacious opinions of the rest of us were absolutely accurate. Didn't you?" Again that stare. "For the likes of us you were in favor of reopening Devil's Island. Isn't that true?"

Refusing to backtrack, I stood there feeling angry and stupid. Stupid because I'd fallen into her neat little trap and angry because I didn't know how to get out of it.

Tracy eased me off the limb.

"Calm down before you split your spleen, Tony. Everybody else got a ride on his garbage wagon. Most of them are boiling mad—the rest of them are dying laughing."

"I fail to see the humor in it!"

"It's hilarious." She struck a hammy pose. "I'm terribly talented, but he said I danced like a duck and sang like a crow. He said Jade was a bovine creature who performed crude awkward routines and wore a wig."

"I refused to even speak to him," said Jade.

"He asked Darlene how much she made 'on the side' every night after the show was over."

"What did Darlene tell him?"

"She called him a son-of-a-dingo-bitch, and told him she could never make as much as his mother did, because everybody knew he'd used his influence to get his mother the best street corner in town."

They both thought that was incredibly funny.

"You people have a strange sense of humor." I didn't try to hide my disgust.

Tracy regarded me with a sour frown.

"You always refer to everybody in this theatre as 'you people' and you always overload the words with contempt." She made a sad clown face and blotted an imaginary tear. "You just don't like us, do you?"

"I don't have to like you," I said. "All I have to do is work with you."

"Why?" asked Jade. "If you are so contemptuous of show business and so damned superior to our people, what are you doing here? Why did you ever degrade yourself by coming to work here? Who twisted your sanctimonious arm?"

It was none of their business, but for some reason I felt I had to vindicate myself. I explained about the mortgage and my mother's immediate need for money. "That's why I'm working here." I said.

Clapping the back of her hand to her brow, she fell back in a hammy pose of outraged virtue. "Oh, my God!" she intoned tragically. "Oh, the pity of it all!" she clutched at her heart and pretended she was going to faint. "The sacrifice supreme. Little Nell is prostituting herself to pay off the mortgage on the old homestead. "Oh, the shame of it all. Oh, may the good Lord have mercy."

"Stop clowning around, Jade." said Tracy. "You know Tony has no sense of humor. He wouldn't laugh at Michelangelo's wrestlers."

She stood up and took the paper cup out of my hand and flipped it into the trash can. In the doorway she paused and said, "Why don't you two bury the tomahawk? If you'd stop playing those nasty games, you might discover you like each other."

"Yeah, like the Hatfields and the McCoys," said Jade with heavy scorn. But she was blushing with embarrassment.

"Don't mind Tracy," I said. "Her heart is in the right place. It's her brain that isn't."

She gave me a dainty smile. "I think you're becoming indoctrinated. That sounded exactly like one of Marc's poison darts." She unhooked her heels and stood up. "It's time to put on the old personality. My public awaiteth."

I walked out into the hall with her. She indicated the paper in my hand. "Letting this kind of tripe upset you, is about as sensible as pounding sand in a rat hole."

In my dressing room, I started to read the article again, then dropped it in the waste basket. No sense pounding sand in a rat hole. I was wryly amused when I realized I'd been thinking in their jargon. It was like thinking in a foreign language.

Despite working in such close proximity with these uneducated people and the necessity of having to mutilate the English language in some of the scenes, I had tried to use correct grammar when I spoke. But each day it became an effort not to fall into their idioms and slangy disjointed way of talking.

Eventually I would come to realize it was as futile as one man hacking away at the creeping vines that spread over, and swiftly obliterate, an unused road in the jungle. The day Marc handed me a musty moth-bally Sultan's costume and I heard myself saying, "I'm not going to wear that facocta thing." I knew I'd lost the struggle.

That day, however, was still quite a distance around a future corner.

Today, I hadn't yet acknowledged defeat. Though there were prescient signs that I was losing ground.

Slowly I was being forced to admit that some of my preconceived opinions were not infallible.

For instance, to me, a burlesque show had always suggested a bacchanalian revel in front of the curtain and unknown depravity behind it. But over the past weeks I had slowly, but grudgingly, discovered that the fleshpots of burlesque were not nearly as fleshy as I had been led to believe.

The chorus girls worked like galley slaves, for a temperamental slave driver. Instead of practicing sexual depravities in their spare time, they practiced dance routines.

The strip women were usually making a costume for the next week's show or rehearsing new scenes with the comics. They had to do a number in each act, plus scenes and running to change wardrobe. Consequently, their prime pastime was looking for an unoccupied chair.

Tracy knocked and said, "Decent?" She came in and said, "Got some bad news for you, Caruso." She made an apologetic gesture. "We were such a smash in the Parisian number, Marc has decided to star us in an Italian extravaganza next week."

"This is not my day." I said. "First that scurvy newspaper article, and now, this."

"I know you think I'm not much of a singer— and you think singing with me debases your professional talent and lowers your social prestige . . . but . . . the die is cast, and you lose."

In a battle of words, Tracy always left her opponent bleeding. But, I decided to try my unfledged skill against her expertise.

"Sometimes you have to bend your principles a little. Mine are beginning to look like a pretzel, so I may as well sing with you and complete the debacle."

"Did anybody ever tell you that you have a close kinship with the hindquarters of a horse?" she asked sweetly.

"No. Did anybody ever tell you that your grandmother was Lucretia Borgia?"

"Touche!" she chortled. "If you're not careful, someday you may join the boys with the cap and bells."

Marc came through the door in time to hear her last remark.

"Not likely," he snapped. "You'd never find a cap big enough, or bells that play, 'How Great Thou Art.'"

"Who starched your shorts?" she purred.

Marc handed me a slip. "This is Vesti La Giugga. You'll do it in the picture number, next week."

"I don't know Vesti La Giugga."

"Well then, learn it!"

"Besides, I'm no opera singer."

"We all know that!" He was in a vile mood.

Tracy attempted to explain something to him.

"Tracy, will you shut up!"

Tracy didn't shut up, but before it reached the mayhem stage, Luttie came prancing in.

"I brought the draw money back." She counted it out to Marc and Tracy and handed them the slips to sign.

She leaned over me and counted out mine while she breathed in my ear and rubbed her pelvis against my arm.

When she gave me the slip to sign, she leaned over closer to give me an unobstructed view of her flabby breasts, which she was sure would arouse my uncontrollable lust.

"Luttie, will you excuse us?" Marc made it a very curt dismissal.

"There ought to be a law against her," I said.

"It's your devastating sex appeal," said Tracy. "Luttie threw up her drawers over the windmill the first time she saw you."

"I'm flattered."

"Will you two would-be comedians get out of here!" yelled Marc.

In the hall we met Joey Benson. He handed Tracy a script. "We'll do this scene next week." As he walked away, Tracy's face had the expression of a man with a king-sized hangover who had just been served a breakfast of boiled fat pork.

"Why does he always pick me for his lousy scenes?" she demanded of a malevolent fate.

"I don't have to worry about being in his scenes," I said. "He doesn't like me at all."

"That's understandable," she said. "If everybody in the theatre who liked you gave you a quarter— you couldn't buy a cup of coffee."

"Am I that bad?"

"No. You're worse."

Luttie came seesawing through the archway and tripped over a coil of rope.

"John, will you get that damned rope out of the way?"

"Aren't you a little out of your territory?" he grated. "You don't have authority to give orders back here."

She whirled and went back toward Barry's office. A minute later, Barry came out and told John to move the rope. He threw the rope over a pin and said with heavy contempt, "If that bitch stepped in shit, Barry Previn would lick her heels."

Slim shrugged and said philosophically "Never underestimate pussy power, my boy. Never underestimate pussy power."

"Please boys," begged Tracy. "Remember Tony's delicate sensibilities. And don't forget I'm a lady." She did a bump on the word lady.

"Tracy, will you do me a favor?" I asked.

"I'll try. What is it?"

"Chou Chou gave me a scene to do next week. Will you rehearse it with me?"

"Sure I'll cue you. But first, I'll have to teach you some of the rudimentary rules."

"Why?"

"Because you do everything wrong."

"Don't I do anything right?"

"Nothing that I've seen so far."

"What's my biggest mistake?"

"Getting into show business," she dead-panned.

"Thanks, Lucretia. I didn't ask for a lecture. I only wanted to learn how to do the scene right."

"That's what I'm going to teach you," she said. "The first rule—you always keep your mind two beats ahead of your tongue. Second rule—you learn your lines. You learn your lines. You learn your lines. Then you learn the lines of everybody that is working in the scene. That's so you'll know what you're talking about. Third rule—Don't chew up the scenery. Don't fall over the furniture. And be sure they hear you in the second balcony."

"All that just to learn some crappy scene?"

"This isn't an acting rule." She put a kindly hand on my shoulder. "This is a survival rule. Don't ever let Chou Chou hear you use the word crappy in connection with one of his scenes."

"Thanks, I'll try to remember."

Marc appeared in the archway. "Tracy, what kind of costume are you going to wear in the jazz number?"

"Two postage stamps and a band-aid."

He jerked his chin toward the stage and said stonily, "Save your comedy for your public. I can do without it!"

He shuffled the music in his hands, and waited.

"If it's an Indian number, I'll wear an Indian costume. If it's a Mexican number, I'll wear a Mexican costume. If it's an Eskimo number, I'll wear an Eskimo costume. All right?"

"And if it's a jockey number, you can be the horse's ass!" He threw the handful of lyrics at her and went striding back to his office.

Listening to them wrangling, I was convinced that actors were somewhere between obstreperous children, Hindu thuggees, and asylum inmates.

Lewis Carrol should have had Alice put her hands against a stage door and push. She would have found a Wonderland filled with stranger, and far more diverse, characters.

Tracy glared at me and said frostily, "Well, do you want to sit there and laugh like an idiot, or do you want to learn how to do the scene?"

"I want to learn how to do the scene."

Strangely enough, I did want to learn how to do the scene. Even though I couldn't get entirely past my personal convictions that all burlesque actors were low class people, I was beginning to like working here. I liked the magic of the theatre. Gradually it had begun to take hold. The lifting excitement of each rising curtain. The frenzy of Marc's pre-show dementia. The intimate world behind the footlights. But most of all, the applause. Nothing can equal the thrill of that third bow.

"Do you want to rehearse up here or in the basement?" she asked.

"In the basement. There's too many diversions up here."

As I followed her down the steps, she turned and glared up at me. "And, for God's sake, learn what timing is!"

"With you as a teacher, how could I miss?"

"With me as a teacher you might learn to be a straight man." Then she said mockingly, "Who knows, someday you might even make it to Broadway—when elephants learn to fly."

BOOK SEVEN

Jade LeMare

My life will not have been lived in vain
If somewhere along my path
When I donned my cap and bells
I made an audience laugh

"Irish"

CHAPTER TWENTY-ONE

Saturday. Another opening day. Another day of trying to "Screw your courage to the sticking place." Somehow, mine always came unstuck. An opening day, added to the recent siege of horrors would unstick the courage of Prince Valiant.

The day had one saving grace. We no longer had to run the gauntlet of vultures at the stage door. Once again we had lost the spotlight. Caralyn, like Aidey, had become old news.

However, my two granite friends still made their daily visits. Although their investigative possibilities seemed to have all been exhausted.

Now we could only sit on the powder keg and wonder how fast the fuse was burning.

Papa Clark teased me about being so early.

"I like to come into the theatre early," I said. "When it's empty and quiet. When only spirits are here."

"You're a pixilated little colleen." He said.

My own spirits lifted as I entered the wings and caught the scent of the freshly scrubbed stage, mingled with the smell of greasepaint and the dusty curtains. They were blended together making the unmistakable aroma of a theatre. As I crossed the big empty stage, I knew it was the most wonderful odor on earth.

Humming "There's no business like show business," I unlocked the padlock, went inside and flipped the light switch. Then froze—fighting back a strange certainty that something was wrong. The back of my neck started to feel prickly, as I picked out the signs of disarrangement here and there.

Someone had been in my dressing room!

But that was impossible. I always carry my own stout padlock with me wherever I go. I have the only key. I moved around the room on a tour of inspection. There was the make-up case slightly out of place. Other things had been moved and the drawer of the secret compartment lacked a fraction of being closed.

Alarm signals started going off when I realized somebody had searched my room—very thoroughly.

I went outside and examined the padlock. It had not been tampered with. Maybe I'm becoming paranoid, I thought. Then I got my magnifying glass. Under the powerful glass, the screw heads showed the clear scratches of a screwdriver. Somebody had removed the hasp, then screwed it securely back in place.

Searching my room could only mean one thing— somebody must suspect me of something. But of what? Knowing something about the murder? Knowing something about the gold? Or both? Most important of all, who was the somebody?

Before I went completely to pieces, I had to know if my room was the only one that had been searched.

I went down the hall inspecting each door hasp with the glass. None had been tampered with. The same routine upstairs.

That left one bald fact. The murderer knew where to look for whatever he was searching for.

Maybe it wasn't the murderer. Maybe it was the police.

When Tracy came in, bringing a cup of tea, I was trying to apply lipstick somewhere in the vicinity of my mouth.

"What's the matter?" she said. "You're shaking like Carrie Finnell's tassels."

"Nothing. Just the usual opening day dementia."

"I'll bet Anne Boleyn wasn't shaking that bad on her way to the guillotine," she jibed.

"Annie didn't have to worry about having to read her press reviews next day."

"Relax. Remember the finale always ends the agony. It's the same old 'off to Buffalo' . . . nothing to worry about."

No there was nothing to worry about—if you didn't count the little things like having your room searched by somebody who was planning to arrest you, or make you his next victim.

Sipping the tea helped a little, but I was still rattling inside like a palsied skeleton.

I went through my number in a state of suspended animation. One hard fact kept time with the music. Very soon I was going to have to tell somebody where a fortune in gold was hidden, and its possible link to murder.

Not the police. I was certain I could never convince my two granite friends that finding that hoard of gold was nothing more that a ten million-to-one fluke.

That left a choice of someone in the theatre. But what if I picked the murderer for my confidant?

The door opened and Dickie came halfway through. "You mus' not heard me knockin'." He regarded me anxiously. "You look kinda scared. Did somethin' bad happen again?"

"Something happened that's got me scared out of my wits."

"What wuz it?"

He knew everything I did about the gold, so I figured I may as well tell him the rest. "Somebody came in here last night and searched my room, and everything in it."

"How could they get in? You always put the padlock on."

"They took the hasp off the door jamb, then screwed it back in place again."

"Was it the one that hurt . . . Aidey an' Caralyn . . . ?" His eyes showed he was frightened.

"It must've been. Who else would have any reason?"

"Why'd they go searchin' in here? What wuz they lookin' for?"

"Maybe somebody suspects we found the gold money? I don't know. Maybe somebody knows more than we do?"

"Did they find our money?" His face puckered up.

His little plush horse with the wheels on its feet was still on the daybed where he left it yesterday.

"No, sweetie, he didn't find our money. We must have a special angel who sends out hunches."

Yesterday, for no tangible reason, I'd used my cuticle scissors to clip the seam stitching in the belly of the little horse. I stuffed the gold pieces into the sawdust and carefully stitched the seam back up again.

That was the only thing that kept me from going berserk, knowing the searcher had found nothing suspicious. The jewel box was still in the trunk drawer. There was no way anybody could know that it hadn't always been mine.

I put my arm around him. "Sweetie, we're going to have to tell somebody about the money we found in that little room, and about the ones you gave Aidey and me. I'm sure somebody already suspects something about it. And I'm almost sure it has something to do with the murders."

"Don't tell th' police, Jade. They'd put us in jail."

"No they won't," I assured him. "I wasn't going to tell them anyway."

"Then who'll ya tell?"

"I've decided to tell Huey. He's the manager. Let him take care of the whole thing."

He fiddled with the comb for a moment. "Arlete says it's a sin to tell lies. She says people that tell lies are bad."

I absorbed that bit of information without quite knowing what to make of it. When I didn't say anything, he swallowed a couple of times and said, "Please don't tell Huey . . . He's a bad person . . . he tells lies."

"He does? What about?"

"Well . . . you know th' night we found Caralyn . . . back there?"

"Yes."

"And 'emember later . . . when you wuz goin' to do your number . . . an' tole me to sit on th' stool an' wait for you?"

"Yes, I remember."

"Well . . . I saw my ball behind the pinrail an' I got off th' stool to go get it."

"Okay, you got down to get your ball."

"Well . . . Huey an' that big cop wuz standing in front of th' pinrail . . . well, I couldn't help from hearin' what they wuz sayin'."

"You were eavesdropping. So, what did you hear?"

"Well . . . the big cop wuz askin' Huey a whole bunch of questions about findin' Caralyn . . . an' Huey said he didn't know what happened at first. He said he wuz out front when he heard you screamin' . . . He said he run down the side aisle and nen he run around behind the backdrop . . . an' he saw you and Barry tryin' to help Caralyn . . ." Dickie stopped for breath. "Well . . . he wuz a tellin' a big lie."

"Why would Huey tell a lie about what he did?"

I don't know, but he did. When you tole me to run fast an' tell Slim . . . I did. An' Barry wuz right there. When he heard you screamin' he went runnin' back there real fast, and I went runnin' back there too."

"I don't know what you're trying to tell me, but you sure are taking a long time."

"Well . . . Huey didn't come runnin' from out front. He wuz right there. He come out of th' wardrobe room."

"That's silly. What would Huey be doing in the wardrobe room in the dark? Are you absolutely sure he didn't come from the other side of the stage?"

"Dammit, Jade! I saw him come out of the wardrobe room!" he said with angry insistence. "He ju' kinda stood there in th' door for a second . . . lookin' down at you an' Barry . . . an' nen he acted like he jus' got there."

Reconstructing the same in my mind, I knew Dickie had to be right. It had taken Barry only a second or two to get there from the switchboard and Huey had arrived only a few seconds later. It would be impossible for him to come from the front of the theatre in that short space of time.

"He'd probably been to the toilet, back there," I said.

"In the dark? An' why would he tell a lie about it?"

I had a hunch, but of course I couldn't explain it to Dickie. Huey probably had been pressing his amorous suit on one of the cutting tables, and being a gentleman, didn't want to expose the lady who had been providing the hot iron. It wouldn't be the first time a cutting table had been used in lieu of hay for a romantic roll.

Why didn't you tell me all this before now?"

"Well . . . Tramp an' Arlete like workin' here. We got a real nice apartment an' ever'thing . . . an' well . . . if I tole anything that made Huey get in trouble, he'd fire Tramp an' Arlete."

Wise little Dickie. He'd been born in the theatre and knew instinctively that having a job was the most important thing in the life of a small time actor. If you want to eat, you have to work. And if you want to work, you learn very early to tread carefully when you're near a manager's toes.

He took my hand and pleaded, "Jade, please le's not tell Huey about the little room or th' money."

"All right, I won't tell him. But we're going to have to tell somebody."

Yes, I knew I had better tell somebody and tell them mighty soon. Also, I'd better choose the right person. Reluctantly, I decided that animated granite statue, Mulchahe, was the most logical choice.

"Jade, how come they didn't find our money?"

"I fed it to 'Getty-up' through a hole in his belly. So don't you touch him. Just leave him there on the bed."

This struck him as being very funny as well as being the best hiding place in the whole world.

Tracy knocked and opened the door. She was wearing a Jester's suit and a belled cap, and carrying a poupart.

"Jeez Chris'" said Dickie. "Ya look like a clown."

"That's what I'm supposed to look like, you dumb-dumb."

"Marc talked me into doing this. It's a circus thing. Everybody is doing back-ups and cartwheels. Penny is doing a tight-rope act. At least she's going to try."

"I hope it turns out better than her rope-twirling act. In that one, she usually looked like she was trying to hang herself."

"You got dirt on your face." Dickie told Tracy.

She used my make-up towel to brush it away. As she was leaving she gave me a wink and said, "That must've come off the listening device."

I started to laugh, but suddenly those two words choked it off. Listening device. What if whoever was in my room had planted one in here? My eyes darted around the room.

"What are you lookin' for?" asked Dickie.

"Nothing. Why don't you go get us a couple of cokes. I'm buying."

I didn't want a coke. I wanted to see if Mulchahe had come backstage yet.

He was leaning against the guardrail watching the actors as they came and went. His expression said he'd seen enough of them to last him the rest of his life.

"Lieutenant Mulchahe . . . could you find a listening device if there was one planted in my room . . .?"

Apparently there was a bad connection between ear and brain. His expression didn't change a hair, but I knew my question had started some wheels turning.

"It's possible," he finally said. "I've been in this line of work for thirty years. I'm beginning to learn a thing or two here and there." The sarcasm wasn't even thinly veiled.

"Good. I'm glad to hear your career is finally shaping up." I turned to leave. To hell with him!

"Wait a minute!" It was a command. "Why would there be a bug planted in your room?"

"There may not be, but I'd like to make sure." My voice trailed off.

"All right, let's go see what we can find."

When he finished, he spread his hands. "Clean as a whistle." He seated himself and fixed me with a frigid stare. "Now what makes you think there might be a bug planted in here?"

I told him about the hasp being taken off the door, and the room being searched.

"Are you sure? How do you know they searched the room?"

"I'm as mechanical as a robot about keeping everything in the same place. Things had been moved and then put back." I gave him the magnifying glass and showed him the marks of the screwdriver. "See, they took the hasp off, then screwed it back in place again."

He looked at me with considerable surprise, but didn't say anything.

I hadn't expected him to praise me as a super sleuth, but I did think he could have given me an approving grunt. We went back inside.

"Have you any idea why anyone would search your room, or want to know what was being said in here."

"I . . . think I have," I faltered. He looked twice as big as Goliath. "I'm not sure, though."

"Very well, this calls for some questions. And this time I would like some intelligent answers."

"Okay. But you'll find out I'm no smarter today than I was the last time you asked me all your questions." When I get intimidated, I tend to get smart alecky.

"Sometimes when people get the hell scared out of them, they smarten up quite a bit." He arranged himself in the old guest chair. "Did they find what they were looking for?"

"No they didn't." I said smugly.

"Then I think you'd better tell me what they were looking for. And why anybody would want to hear what you say in here?"

"It's a long involved rigmarole and I have a tendency to pad my part."

"I have plenty of time."

"Okay. I'll hit the high spots. Since I first came here Dickie has been trying to bribe me out of a little knife. One day he came in and offered to buy it with some pretty new stage money he'd found. The stage money turned out be a very old twenty dollar gold piece.

"Finally he confessed he'd had another one. He gave it to Aidey the night of the party. That same night Aidey was murdered and the gold piece disappeared. Dickie said she put it in her pocket. She didn't leave the theatre that night, and the gold piece isn't in her pocket."

"How do you know?"

"Dickie and I both looked. Her coat is hanging in the prop room."

"Go on."

I bribed Dickie into telling me where he found the gold pieces, then I persuaded him to show me where."

You always dramatize the punchline, so I paused, then said, "There were a lot more of them. In fact, there's about a million dollars in twenty dollar gold pieces hidden up there!"

I had expected the punchline to floor him. It was like expecting the Mona Lisa to frown.

"Where's 'up there' where all this gold is hidden?"

Dickie entered just in time to hear the question. He stared at Mulchahe and said, "Don't tell him, Jade. He'll put us in jail!"

"No, he won't." I reassured him.

"Well, go on," prompted Mulchahe.

"If you go out into the auditorium and look up to the left, you'll see a gridwork camouflaged with a lot of grubby cherubim. There's an old organ chamber behind it. The gold is in there."

"That's silly, Jade. He can't get up there from out front."

"I know that. He probably can't get up there from back here, either. He'd pull the ladder right out of the wall."

"He'd prolly pull the catwalk down," chortled Dickie.

Our comedy routine wasn't amusing the lieutenant. This time his question had an edge to it.

"Now, how do you get up there where the gold is hidden?"

"On the other side of the stage there's an iron ladder that goes up to the fly loft. You have to climb that," I said meekly. Pitching comedy at a policeman is like preaching platitudes to a mole.

"How did this kid happen to find all that gold?" He still sounded very skeptical.

I explained about Dickie's fascination with his magnet and how he came to find the cache. "The odds are about ten million to one that anyone would ever slide a magnet over that one little spot."

His shrug indicated the odds were rather trifling. "Any idea how it got up there?"

"Oh, yes! But I don't guarantee it to be the right one."

He shifted to a more comfortable position and waited.

"I think a skinny little old miser carried it up there. Maybe forty or fifty years ago." I gave him a run-down on old man Rozen and his chain of theatres that always showed such meager profits.

"How did you find out about all this, at such a late date?"

"Slim told me. He said there were a lot of rumors when the old man died, that he had hidden all his money in this old theatre. He said after all these years everybody had forgotten all about them. Besides, nobody had ever really believed them. But after seeing Dickie's gold pieces—I did!"

He looked at Dickie. "Why did you want to climb up that ladder?"

"We ain't got no trees back stage."

Mulchahe pretended he didn't hear him. He turned back to me. "And you think there's some connection between you two finding the gold and your room being searched?"

"Yes, I do! And I think it has something to do with both murders, too!" I curled my lip and said, "And I don't give a damn whether you think I'm silly, or not!"

"And you think one person committed both murders?"

"Yes. I think the same person committed both murders!"

"Did you ever see this Caralyn talking to the other girl?"

"That big stupid klutz! No never. That would've been like Einstein trying to discuss relativity with the village idiot."

He inspected me with a dubious frown. "In that case, then what would be the connection?"

"I don't know. Aidey was strangled and her gold piece disappeared. Caralyn was strangled in the same way. But she didn't have a gold piece."

"Yes, she did," said a small quavering voice behind me. "I gived her one because she brought me a little toy car."

"Oh, holy herkermer, Dickie! Why didn't you tell me you had filched a carload of the things?"

"I didn't know it wuz real money, Jade. Not then . . ."

I looked at Mulchahe and said, "I'm just as surprised as you are."

I'm not surprised." He said impassively. "Nothing you two do would surprise me." He nodded a go-ahead at me.

"Finding out Caralyn had a gold piece makes it a bit more complicated. I'm certain Aidey had no idea where Dickie got the coin, but I think Caralyn knew as soon as she saw it."

"What makes you so certain."

"Because her grandmother's picture is tacked to the wall in the room where the gold is hidden." I said, and watched another punchline fall as flat as a Sunday matinee in Seattle.

"Caralyn Ayres' grandmother?"

"That's right. Caralyn Ayres' grandmother."

I knew Mulchahe was intrigued despite his pretended skepticism. In that case, I might as well go for the Oscar award.

"Fifty years ago there was a beautiful singer on Broadway. Fifty years ago it was rumored that old man Rozen had a beautiful mistress. Shortly after old man Rozen died the beautiful singer dropped out of existence. Fifty years later a beautiful girl turns up to sing at the Empress burlesque theatre. She needed to work in a burlesque theatre like Galli-curci needed to work the Gus Sun Time."

"That's very interesting."

"Just interesting? I thought it was brilliant."

"Caralyn Ayres was too young to be the daughter of Gaby LeGere, but she was just the right age to be her granddaughter. And the granddaughter of old man Rozen. Let's say grandmother Gaby told granddaughter Caralyn about the gold her grandfather had hidden somewhere in this old theatre, and it had never been found. That would be a mighty good reason for her to come here to work. Gold is a powerful magnet."

Mulchahe studied the smutchy ceiling and chewed his lip.

"You know," he admitted grudgingly. "All these fanciful speculations of yours are beginning to make sense."

"Thank you. We both thank you, don't we, Dickie?"

"Are you sure you and this kid are the only ones that know anything about that place up there?"

"Absolutely sure. We're the only ones." I gave him a prima donna smile. "And as a reward for our clever Sherlocking, would you make sure that our friendly neighborhood murderer doesn't present Dickie and me with a pair of complimentary trickline necklaces?"

He sighed as though my farce was more than he could stand.

Frankly, I had been overdoing the hyperbole. But, like Scheherazade, I was afraid to run out of stories.

"Don't worry," he said. "I can't afford to let anything happen to you two. You're the only ones that can show me where all that gold is hidden."

"Jeez Chris'!" erupted Dickie. "I ain't never goin' to go back up that place no more."

"We'll see, when the time comes." Mulchahe said.

Besides," said Dickie angrily. "You can't go goin' up there.

There's a whole bunch of them old cigar boxes up there an' the money's in them. I'f you go up there and start carryin' all them boxes down the ladder . . . . well then . . . the murderer . . . he'll guess what's in 'em . . . an' then you take 'em all away, he'll know the gold is gone . . . an' he'll quit lookin' for it . . . an' nen you won't ever know who he is."

Mulchahe looked at me and shook his head disbelievingly.

I know that—but how did *he* figure it out so quick."

"Just smart, I guess."

"I wasn't planning to do that, anyway," he said. "I know you have to leave the bait in the trap if you want to catch the game."

"How will you know when he finds it? How will you spring the trap?"

"It will depend on how things go."

"For instance?"

"We'll have to wait and see. In the meantime, I don't want you and the kid to tell a soul anything about that room."

"Don't worry. We won't."

"I didn't even tell Tramp an' Arlete," said Dickie.

See that you don't." He stressed the words.

He stood up but seemed reluctant to go.

Catching his indecision, I wondered if he really believed my unbelieveable story. It was so incredible, I could hardly believe it myself.

As everyone knows, actors are likely to pad their parts with a bit of fantasy.

I once worked with an off-center straightman. One day he was chewing his lip and shaking his head in a worried manner. I asked him what was wrong.

"I wish I could find those deeds." He said dolefully.

"What deeds?" I foolishly asked.

My grandfather left me the deeds to all the property that downtown Philadelphia is built on," he said. "But I've mislaid them somewhere."

Then there was the singer who was the reincarnation of an Egyptian princess. She'd show you her hands to prove it. Each had a ring that had been reincarnated along with her.

Then there was the comic who always wore white. He insisted he was Jesus Christ.

Then there was Jade claiming she had discovered the Lost Dutchman Mine.

I started laughing.

"What's funny?" Mulchahe asked.

"Actors in general. Me in particular." I said. "We're all pixilated."

"I'll go along with that." He actually grinned.

At the door, he said, "You and the kid be careful."

That's when I began to wonder if deep down inside, the animated block of granite didn't have a soft core—something called a heart.

CHAPTER TWENTY-TWO

I wasn't asleep, nor entirely awake. I was somewhere in between struggling to elude the menacing coils of trickline that had snaked after me in my dreams.

Opening my eyes would banish the last remnant of the nightmare.

Keeping them closed would delay the beginning of a new day. A new day of wondering if, once again, Charon would be found lurking in the wings with his paddles at the ready.

And, if this should be the day, who would be his next fare?

Burying my head under the pillow, I considered calling the theatre to say I'd been stricken with the plague. But, since I'm an old hand with compromising with myself, I got up and began getting dressed to go to work.

After all, the show must go on.

This is the first commandment of show business, and most actors pay it strict obedience. Occasionally a callow amateur will cynically ask "Why?"—while busily putting on his make-up.

Being the conscientious breed of actor, I keep this first commandment faithfully. I never miss a show if it is humanly possible to be there. Although it could be that what I have always felt was true dedication to my art, is, in reality, an over-quotient of Smithfield.

Whichever, I would trade the pearly gates for a stage door anytime. And the heavenly host for a midnight audience.

To an actor, giving a bang-up performance and hearing the resultant applause, far outranks a harp and a crown.

The actor's day dawns when the curtain rises. The spotlight is his morning sun. The reaction of the audience is his emotional barometer. He feeds his soul on their adulation. An actor loves the theatre. The theatre is his castle. And the stage door is the magic portal through which he travels from beggar to king.

Ah yes, the show must go on, but for the sake of the actor, not the audience.

Papa Clark opened the magic portal and I became a queen.

When I crossed the stage, I was surprised to find my granite friend encamped on one of the stools by the switchboard. I was even more surprised to find he was in an affable mood. Not only was he affable, he was downright waggly-tailed friendly; like a big benign wolf waiting to share the goodies in Little Red Ridinghood's basket.

"What are you doing here so early?" I asked. "And where is your partner?"

"He stopped for a sandwich. He'll be along."

"Has he changed his spots, too?"

"I beg your pardon . . ."

"Nothing. It's too early for jokes."

He looked at my face. "You look kinda hollow-eyed this morning."

"Yeah, I know. Jade and the Golden Fleece. This treasure hunt is costing me a lot of sleepless nights."

He clucked sympathetically.

"I wish you'd hurry up and find out who-done-it." I said. "Knowing the murderer is still walking around back here is rather hard on the nerves. Especially since he's been walking around in my dressing room."

"We'll try to catch him before you go off on another one of your treasure hunts."

I stuck my tongue out at him.

Dickie came in with Tramp and Arlete and received a "Good Morning, Peck's Bad Boy,"as he went by.

My, my, Mister Friendly was wagging his tail at Dickie! Seemingly our stock had gone up like a bull market.

Being a shade smarter than he gave me credit for, I was almost sure I knew what had brought about the change. Telling him where about a million dollars worth of evidence was hidden had mellowed my granite friend considerably. Even if he was a little dubious of my story.

After doing a bit of subtle, but unsuccessful, fishing, I gave up and asked boldly, "Do you have any suspects?"

"I have a couple of prime candidates."

"How will you . . . what are you going to do?"

"I'm going to set a bear trap."

"I suppose you wouldn't . . . ?" I left the question hanging.

"That's right. I wouldn't."

"What happens if neither one of them is the right one?"

"I'll bet my badge one of them is the right one."

"I'll take that bet—I'll put up my rhinestone G-string." I said as I left.

By the time I came out for my number, O'Brien was there.They were watching a re-run of two grunting Neanderthals knocking each other's brains out. They were still there after the finale, but now, they were sitting on the stools in a deep conversation.

During the second act, I was busy sewing sequins on my new Oriental costume, when Dickie came in and announced he was going to have dinner with me.

"Did Tramp and Arlete say you could?"

"Naw, but they will when I ask 'em. They always do."

"That's because you eat so much they're glad to have somebody else feed you."

"I'll see ya after the show," he said with a pained grimace. "If I stick aroun' here, I might die laughin'."

After the last finale I got into my street clothes and sat down to sew more sequins while I waited for him.

Gradually I became aware the theatre had grown quiet. I'd been so engrossed in the costume I hadn't noticed the time. I opened my door and called, then went down the hall to their room. The door was locked. I assumed they had said he couldn't go, so I put on my coat and boots and locked my door. I wondered why he hadn't come back to tell me be couldn't go.

Apparently everyone had gone. The front curtain was up and all the lights were out, except the work light upstage.

Crossing the stage, I heard a curious muffled sound. I thought it was probably the echo of my own footsteps. But when I paused, the sound didn't stop. I stood very still and listened, trying to detect where the thumping was coming from. Then suddenly I caught my breath and looked upward. The sound was coming from the fly loft.

Who, or what, could be thumping around up there? No stage hands ever worked up there anymore. All the ropes that used to be worked from the flys, were now controlled from the pinrail.

"Probably Old Man Rozen is carrying away his gold." I told myself facetiously.

Despite my levity, an uneasy feeling began gathering in the pit of my stomach as I continued walking across the stage. I am very allergic to ghosts. Then, barely audible, I thought I heard Dickie call my name. I stopped directly below the catwalk and stood listening. He called again!

That little imp of Satan! He had climbed back up there again. In my mind's eye I could see him clinging to the rail, too terrified to climb back down by himself. I was mad enough to bat him one when I got my hands on him.

I left my purse and coat on the floor, at the foot of the ladder and cursing my frustrated mother complex, I started to climb. My lungs had collapsed and my arms had turned into boiled noodles by the time I pulled myself up onto the catwalk.

I saw him halfway back, huddled against the railing; his face startlingly white in the murky half-light. I crawled over on my hands and knees and grabbed his arms.

"You incorrigible little brat!" I said. "What in the hell are you doing up here again?" I backed toward the top of the ladder, trying to drag him with me, but he wouldn't let go of the railing. He seemed frozen there in abject terror.

"Come on, you awful brat." I tugged at him. "Let's go!"

"We can't go, Jade." he whimpered. "He won't let us. He made me call you. He said if I didn't . . . he'd throw me over the railing. He knows you know about the money."

Instant realization. Then paralyzing panic. The murderer had brought Dickie up here, then used him to get me up here.

There was a slight movement farther back on the catwalk.

I turned my head and saw Huey standing near the small door. For one heartbeat, my reaction was one of overwhelming relief. Then I saw the length of trickline. He was holding it in his right hand and sliding it through his left palm—almost as if it were a living thing and he was caressing it.

"Sorry." I heard his pleasant voice saying, "but I'm afraid you two can't go just yet.

For a moment I had the strange sensation of being wide awake while deep in the terrors of a nightmare. But nightmares were peopled with ghouls and hideous beasts. This one only had Huey. And the most chilling part of it was the lack of any change in him. He still looked nice and kind and genial. He still had the same lilt of laughter in his voice. The only incongruous thing about him was the length of trickline in his hands.

I stared at him, appalled. "Huey? Oh, my God, Huey. It can't be you. It can't be you."

"Yes, I'll have to admit it's me," he laughed. Then shook his head as he stood staring down at us.

"For years I've been trying to figure out where that old coot could've stashed his fortune." He seemed overcome with astonishment.

"I've stayed here a good many nights and searched every crack and crevice in this old theatre. Then along comes a very lucky little girl, who manages to find it in only a few short weeks." He played with the deadly rope. "Who—or what—put you onto it? How did you find out about it—and how did you find it?"

I shook my head, trying to unfuzz my thoughts. "I didn't find it. Dickie did. He thought it was stage money. One day he gave me one. When he gave Aidey one, I made him show me where he found it."

"I really don't care which one of you found it." He smiled his charming smile. "All I want to know, is, where is it now?" he nodded toward the small door. "Dickie says it's in the old organ chamber— but he can't seem to remember where."

He motioned for us to stand up, then he opened the door and stood aside for us to enter. I let Dickie go first, then ducked my head and stepped in behind him.

And stopped dead!

Standing in the midst of the organ pipes was that ugly pop-eyed toad—Old Hot Crotch Steiner!

"Surprise! Surprise! She mocked and pulled down the corners of her flat mouth. "Imagine finding me here." Her feral little teeth glinted behind her smirk.

My mind fleetingly registered her malevolent toad face and heard her gloating words, but my eyes were glued to the iron pry bar she held in her hands. It was more murderous looking than the rope in Huey's hands.

Huey was whistling a tune from the Student Prince while he let his eyes wander over the chamber.

"Huey, will you hurry this up?" croaked the toad. "We don't have forever, you know."

"Well, anybody can see there's no place here where you could hide a piggy bank." He smiled with a flash of white teeth and said persuasively, "So, where have you and Dickie been getting those pretty twenty dollar gold pieces?"

There was nothing to be gained by stalling.

"They're behind the wall over there." I waved in the general direction. "There's a panel that opens."

Then get your ass over here and open it!" commanded the toad.

"You have to have a magnet to get it open."

"A magnet?" she sneered. "What kind of a crock of shit is that? Who do you think you're kidding?"

Dickie tugged at my hand and I leaned down so he could whisper in my ear.

"I ain't got my magnet with me," he said, sobbing silently.

"Come on, kiddies," chided Huey. "No secrets."

"Dickie doesn't have his magnet. You have to have a magnet to find the panel," I repeated. "That's how he happened to find it in the first place."

"Well, which one is it?" Toad-face hefted the pry bar. "We can break the fucking thing in with this."

"I can't possibly remember which one it is," I stammered. Fear was making me incoherent. "They all look alike."

"Maybe this will help you remember." She raised the pry bar and came a step closer.

"I can't remember!" I cried hysterically.

"But you can remember Aidey and Caralyn, can't you?"

"Why did you have to murder them?" I couldn't control my voice, or the tears. Why. . . ?"

"Because they couldn't remember anything, either," said Huey. "They both kept stalling. No matter how hard I tried, I couldn't make make them tell me where they got the gold pieces." He shrugged and smiled.

"Of course, you can understand why I couldn't leave them alive to tell the police what it was I wanted to know." He held the trickline in his right hand and snaked it through his left. "Or the methods I used trying to make them tell."

"How did you know it was Dickie that found the money?"

"Luttie did a lot of eavesdropping backstage."

Asking questions was only a desperate attempt to delay the inevitable moment when Dickie and I would be thrown over the railing. Once they had exposed their cards, the game was over.

But, like a drowning man clutching at a straw, I had to go on asking questions.

"How did you get Aidey to go up on that platform?"

"She was sitting on the bench with her eyes leaking. I kidded her until she stopped sniffling. When she reached into her pocket for a tissue, something fell out. When I saw what it was, I was sure I knew where it had come from."

I went to Barry's office and typed a note on his memo pad telling her to meet him up there. I told her Barry had asked me to slip her the note when Luttie wasn't around. Then I went to the prop room and hid behind some scenery. Three minutes later, Aidey was climbing that ladder like it was the stairway to heaven," he laughed. "She didn't have enough sense to wonder why he would ask me to deliver his note."

"Is Barry Previn in on this?"

"Hell no!" sneered Toadface. He's peanuts compared to the pot of gold Huey's gonna split with me." She couldn't resist bragging about her fatal sexual prowess. "Huey's been chasing me ever since I've been here. Course I let him catch me real often."

She did a lewd grind to get her point across.

When Huey found out somebody back there had found a couple of gold pieces, he promised to split with me if I'd help him find out who it was. And now we know!" she crowed.

"Luttie, my love," admonished Huey. "You talk too much."

"What difference does it make? They're never gonna tell anybody."

Her meaning was horrifyingly clear. Even to Dickie. He clung to my hand and sobbed, "Jade, don't let them hurt us like they did Aidey an' Caralyn . . . les' get my magnet an' show 'em how to find the stuff."

I couldn't tell him that giving them the magnet would never make any difference in the end.

"We can always get a fucking magnet and find the plate." grated Luttie. "Let's get this over with, Huey—and get the hell outta here." She swaggered around the pipes toward us with the pry bar raised.

I turned my eyes from her just in time to see Huey dropping the loops over my face. I caught them with my fingers before he could jerk the hitch tight. My fingers kept it from cutting into my throat. I screamed once. Then there was a stunning blow against my temple and through waves of blackness, I saw the toad swing the pry bar at Dickie's head.

As I blacked out entirely I had a faint impression of some-one shouting.

CHAPTER
TWENTY- THREE

Pain, like a locomotive thundering through my head, pulled me up out of the blackness, I tried to focus my blurred vision on the people around me. It was no use. They bobbed and weaved like amateur chorus girls trying to find their place in line.

The first one to emerge hazily and stand still, was the most beautiful face in the world. How could I ever have thought that Mulchahe's face wasn't beautiful?

When my vision cleared and everything came into focus, I saw Huey and the toad standing against the wall, being guarded by a large gun in O'Brien's hand.

Their wrists were handcuffed behind their backs.

Surely, I was in some strange fantasy where nothing was real. In no way could I relate the real Huey, with his whimsical humor, his smiling eyes, and his infectious laugh, with the cold-blooded killer standing there beside that malignant toad. When he caught my eye, he gave a philosophical shrug and smiled.

Luttie was glaring at him, her face twisted into a mask of vengeful fury. The fortune in gold he'd promised her, had turned into a death sentence. She had discarded her grovelling slave and his penny ante stake to gamble for much higher stakes, and lost.

Murder is a dangerous game. You're only allowed one mistake.

Whatever their mistake had been, it was clear— judging by the toad's face—that she blamed Huey for the fatal predicament they were in, now.

I pushed myself to a sitting position and saw I was covered with layers of black dust from the floor. The slightest movement sent clouds of the stuff swirling around me.

The sound of a hiccupping sob made me turn my head to look for Dickie. He was sitting on the floor near me, covered with the same black grime, catching his breath in terrified sobs.

I struggled to my feet and made a lunge for Luttie.

"You vicious slut! You tried to murder Dickie. You hit him with that iron bar." I was screaming in a mindless rage as I wound my hands in her hair and began trying to pound her face into a bloody pulp against the wall.

Mulchahe pulled me away from her. Although he didn't seem to be in too great a hurry.

"Take it easy," he said. "The little guy is okay. He's scared half to death, and he's going to have a knot on his noggin for awhile, but he's all right." He grunted something that sounded like a chuckle. "Our entrance put her off her aim. She only caught him a glancing blow."

Dickie stood up and wobbled over to me and took my hand. "Them mean son-a-bitchin' bassards!" he hiccupped.

The toad shot him a look of savage hatred.

Murdering another human being had always been incomprehensible to me. But now, looking at that reprehensible little toad, I realized how easily I could have slammed her brains out against that wall without a single qualm.

Suddenly a wave of wooziness started at my knees and washed up to my head. I sat back down. Dickie stirred up a cloud of the black grime as he came and scrunched down beside me.

Mulchahe nodded toward the two standing against the wall and said, "They went for the bait like a bear going for the bee tree." He seemed extremely pleased with himself.

A sudden suspicion threatened to rupture my skull.

"What bait was that?" I asked.

"Oh, I just happened to let the little broad overhear me telling O'Brien that the kid had found a whole cache of twenty dollar gold pieces." He grinned happily. "I knew Dickie would be mighty tempting bait, if I'd picked the right suspects."

"You lousy stinking cop!" I yelled up at him, "You set us up like a couple of clay pigeons!"

"Now, now," he soothed. "We were at the top of the ladder before Huey took you inside. After that we were right outside the door all the time."

"Then why in the hell didn't you come right *inside* the door. What were you waiting for?"

"We wanted to catch them red handed. We needed to hear what they had to say." He grunted, not quite a chuckle. "We had to give them enough rope to hang themselves."

"Did it ever occur to you that those two ghouls damn near killed us while you were standing around playing out your rope?"

He put two ham-like hands under my arms, lifted me up and stood me on my feet. "Nice girls don't swear," he said.

He lifted Dickie and stood him on his feet. Dickie had quit crying and was wiping the tears through the grime on his face.

"You are being a mighty brave little boy." Mulchahe told him.

"Bullshit, Little Eva!" snarled Dickie.

Mulchahe looked at the two by the wall. "Looks like I only lost half my badge."

"Half?"

"Yeah, I thought the other half of this team would be her lover, Barry Previn."

"I didn't know who it was, but I never dreamed it could be Huey."

There was a long four bar silence, Then, Huey said, "My parents were working here when that old miser died. All we heard was talk about how many millions he had squirreled away. Everybody was sure it was in this theatre. As the years went by, everybody forgot about those old tales. But I didn't. My whole ambition in life was to find that money. It became an obsession. I've searched every crack and rathole a thousand times." He lifted his shoulder in a fatalistic shrug. "When I knew they had found a lot of gold coins—well, I guess I went a little crazy. I knew I'd never let someone else get that gold."

"Jeez Chris'," whined Dickie. "Give him the ole money, les go. I'm starvin' to death!"

Old Hot Crotch opened her mouth, but fear had frozen her vocal cords.

O'Brien choked and coughed. "Can't we finish all this down on the stage? Everybody is kicking up enough dust to choke you." He herded Huey and Luttie out onto the catwalk and we followed them.

Mulchahe started down the ladder.

"Wait a minute," I said. "Let Dickie and me go down first."

O'Brien said, "These two can't climb down that ladder with handcuffs on. How'll they get down?"

"Hellsfire," said Dickie. "Push 'em over the railin'."

I clung to the railing and backed down far enough for Dickie to start.

"Okay, kid. Down you go," said Mulchahe.

"I can't!" wailed Dickie. "I'm afraid. I'll fall!" He was clutching the iron rail with a death grip.

"Well, we can't leave you up here." He attempted to force his hands loose.

"Jade! Jade!" screamed Dickie. "Make him stop!"

I went back up the ladder, yelling, "Leave him alone! Can't you see he's scared?"

"Shut up!" barked Mulchahe. "Shut up and get back down that ladder."

I went back down the ladder.

He pulled Dickie's hands away from the rail. "Okay, now, turn around and put your foot on the rung. I'm holding you real tight. I won't let you fall."

He eased him down until his hands could grasp the first rung. "Okay, keep going, she won't let you fall."

When we stepped off the ladder onto the stage, I yelled, "We're down."

He came swiftly down and stepped off onto the stage. "I'm sorry I had to get so rough," he said. "But you were getting hysterical. Another minute and we'd have to call for a basket to get you two down from up there."

"I know. I know. And you're more than forgiven."

He took a lethal looking gun out of his holster and called, "All right, O'Brien, send than down."

"I'll have to take these cuffs off," bellowed O'Brien. "They can't climb down the ladder with their hands behind their backs."

"Take them off," said Mulchahe. "They're not going any-where." He stood waiting with his gun in his hand.

I tilted my head back and squinted up into the murky light. I could barely make out some movements on the catwalk.

Then there was a bloodcurdling scream of mortal terror as Luttie came hurtling down, with arms flailing and hands grabbing and clawing at the empty air. The screams were cut off like a switch pulled on a blackout when her body crashed onto the stage.

A split second later, she was followed by a silently somer-saulting body that crashed a scant two feet from her shapeless form. Huey hadn't made a sound.

For a mindless eon, we were held frozen in speechless horror. Then O'Brien came backing down the ladder with the sound of metal clanging against metal. When he turned around, he had his gun in his hand.

None of us moved. Mulchahe and O'Brien stood like two amateur actors who had forgotten their lines. The huge guns were merely props for the scene. But it seemed silly to go on holding the drawn guns when the other actors had already ended the scene.

Dickie wouldn't let go of my hand. And he wouldn't look toward the grotesque shapes only a dozen steps away. Their faces were smashed; blood was beginning to ooze from their mouths and nostrils. Their wide staring eyes accused each other.

Finally he tugged at my hand and quavered. "Jade . . . I . . . didn't . . . I . . . didn't mean it when I tole that big cop to push 'em over the railin'. I know I said it, but honest to God . . . I didn't mean it . . . for real."

"I know you didn't. You were just mad at them."

"He didn't push 'em over 'cause I tole him to, did he?"

"He wouldn't push them over because you told him to," I said. "It's not your fault, honey."

"Good God!" O'Brien said, as if he couldn't believe his ears. "Are you two crazy? I didn't push them over that railing!"

He looked at Mulchahe. "I took the cuffs off her first. Then as soon as I took them off him, he reached down, grabbed her by the ankles and flipped her over the rail. Before I could move he leaned against the rail and flipped himself over backwards."

"I don't care how they got down here," I said. "Just as long as Dickie doesn't think it was his fault." I was too near hysteria to have any coherent thoughts or rational feelings. I was only aware of one emotion. I was glad those two mangled bodies lying there so still and lifeless were Huey Ryan and Luttie Steiner, instead of Dickie Dougan and Jade LeMare.

They, who had planned to murder us, were dead. And I was glad.

There is a morbid fascination about death. I had been forcing myself to look at everything on the stage, except those two bloody masses there on the floor. Despite a determined effort not to look, my eyes turned once again toward the grisly sight.

I ran toward the rear of the stage.

"Where are you going?" demanded Mulchahe.

"The wardrobe racks has sheets spread over them to keep the dust off." I returned with the sheets and handed them to him.

"You do it, please."

He covered the shapeless masses and started giving O"Brien instructions. "Call the coroner and tell him to make it on the double. We've got to get these bodies out of here. Have the station send over some uniformed officers to keep order."

"Some one ought to tell the Gruesome Twosome," I said.

"The what?"

"The owners."

"I know their numbers," said Dickie. "I mem'rized 'em from list'nin when Huey used to call 'em."

O'Brien took out his pad and pencil and copied down the numbers. "Do you have an outside phone?" he asked.

"No," said Dickie. "It's over there in the hall."

I looked around the old theatre. "This will probably be the straw that broke the camel's back. This time they'll crucify us."

"Don't you worry about it. I would not let anything happen to you", Mulcahe said.

"I've been under the impression that actors were not your favorite kind of people."

"Oh, they're all right." Something that could have been a smile crossed his face. "Once you get to know them."

"How did you know we were in danger?"

"We've had you and the kid under surveillance every minute since your room was searched and you told me about that gold."

"I didn't much think you believed me."

"I didn't much," he said. "But we couldn't afford to take any chances."

"Were you surprised when you saw it was Huey?"

"That's the understatement of the year."

When one of us moved, the work light upstage sent long ghostly shadows weaving toward the footlights.

"Do you know how to turn on the lights out here?"

"Yes."

When I didn't move, he said, "Well, would you please turn them on?"

"No. It's awful enough when you can barely see. The fullups would make it unbearable."

A shadow moved in front of the orchestra pit, and a moment later as he came up the steps, I recognized Barry. He gaped at our strange little group in puzzled silence.

"If you're looking for the little broad you meet back here after every matinee—she's right here." O'Brien took a step and pulled the sheet from Luttie's body.

It was a cruel, cruel act. The kind of shock that kills a man and let's him go on living. He stared down at her in dumbstruck horror. Silently, he folded down beside her and took her little clawlike hand in his. His hoarse choking sobs echoed in the stillness. He made a motion toward the other sheeted form.

O' Brien removed the sheet. Barry lifted his head and stared up at us. His eyes had the same glazed opaque look as the two on the floor. Through his sobs he said, "Please tell me what happened."

Mulchahe and O'Brien replaced the sheets but offered no answer to his agonized plea. Their only reaction to his flood of tears, was undisguised scorn.

He stood up and put his hand on my arm. "Jade . . . what happened? Why are they. . . ? Sobs choked off his words.

"They're not worth crying over, Barry. They murdered Aidey and Caralyn. They were going to kill Dickie and me."

"You're all crazy. My little darling would never hurt anybody." He couldn't stop sobbing.

Watching a man tear his heart out over a piece of sewer garbage that made a common whore look like your sainted aunt; you find your sympathy tends to be watered down quite a bit with disgust.

"Why don't you stop being such a stupid fool? She was only playing you for a cover-up. She's been Huey's bed partner ever since she's been here. She was a vicious trollop who would kill anybody to get her hands on a lot of money. And, right now, I hope she's roasting over a slow fire in Hell!"

Mulchahe caught my arm and shushed my hysterical tirade.

"I'm sorry, but this is more than I can stand. It's all so horrible. Mulchahe, will you take us out of here?" I pleaded. "Please take us to the hotel."

"I'll have you there in no time at all. He started giving O'Brien orders. "Don't give out any information. Just say there is none available at this time. Get the morgue crew here on the double. Call for a couple of uniforms, just in case we need them to keep order. Call the hotel and tell them to have a doctor there as soon as possible."

Then he turned to Barry, "You weren't here. So, you don't know what happened. Is that understood?" He barked. "Just go home and keep your mouth shut."

Barry nodded silently.

The clerk said the doctor would be there in a few minutes. He was asking questions as we got into the elevator and went up to my room.

"I'm going to scrub this grime off Dickie and myself and then lie down and try to relax. You'd better call Tramp and Arlete and explain what has happened. You can explain better than I can. . ." Then the realization of what their reactions would be hit me like a bolt of lightning. "Oh, my God!" I cried. "They'll faint when they find out how close I came to getting Dickie killed!"

Dickie erupted into a fit of wailing. "Tramp'll whip me!"

"No he won't," soothed Mulchahe. "I'll tell him how you helped us catch those two. "They'll be so proud of you, they'll bust their buttons."

Dickie was half asleep when he came out of the bathroom. I gave him one of my pajama tops and he crawled into bed.

I scrubbed off my own layers of grime and washed my hair. I was wrapped in a robe when the doctor arrived.

He examined us carefully and said we were suffering more from shock than any serious injury. "I'll give you something to calm you down, so you can have a good sleep. You'll be just fine in the morning."

He painted some gunk on the bruise over Dickie's eye and gave him a shot in the arm, which caused Dickie to call him a mean old doctor.

He lifted my hair and touched the bruise on my temple.

"That's a nasty one," he said. "What did you get hit with?"

"A blackjack," said Mulchahe.

The doctor pushed up my sleeve and gave me a shot of the stuff he'd given Dickie. It must have been powerful. Within minutes, I was floating happily on a pink cloud.

He nodded at Dickie. "Is he your son?"

"No, he's a leprechaun. He knows how to find the places where lots of golden treasures are hidden."

The doctor told Mulchahe we'd be all right in the morning and left rather hurriedly.

I sucked in a deep breath. There was something I had to get settled before my gray matter got too mushy.

"Lieutenant Mulchahe, please don't tell anybody anything about that money up there."

"I didn't see any money."

"Take my word for it—it's up there."

He raised an inquiring eyebrow. "Are you planning to file a claim on it?"

Don't be silly," I yawned. "I already got enough."

"You did?"

"Yes, six pieces . . . and Dickie gave me one. I gave him four pieces . . . but I don't know how many he mined on his first trip up there."

"You realize you can't keep this a secret—not after today.

"Why not?"

"For one thing, I have to make a report."

"You can't report where the gold is hidden because you don't know," I yawned. "You don't even know for sure it's even up there . . . and nobody else knows, either!"

"Herlick and Nathan aren't stupid. When I tell them what happened, it won't take them too long to figure out that those two didn't get you and the kid up there to have a picnic. And they can surely figure that people don't murder other people and then kill themselves, unless there's a mighty big prize at stake."

"So let them figure. . ."

"They've got some powerful attorneys. They might take it to court."

"So what? Who're they going to sue? A seven-year-old comic and a dumb strip woman?" I scoffed. "Besides, wouldn't it be a little like suing for the salvage rights to the Flying Dutchman?"

He gave me a pained smile, then said seriously, "I'd advise you to tell them where the money is, and get this thing all settled."

"No. I won't tell them anything."

This time he looked puzzled. "Why not? What have you got to gain?"

"For me, nothing. But, Dickie found the stuff . . . and I won't tell them anything at all, unless they sign an agreement to put fifty thousand dollars in a trust fund for him, so he can go to college when he grows up."

"Fifty thousand dollars is a lot of money."

"Trading fifty thousand for a million and maybe a lot more, sounds like smart horse trading to me."

"What if they refuse to sign this agreement of yours?"

"Then there never was any hidden gold. Dickie found an old purse with two gold pieces in it. He gave one to Aidey and one to Caralyn. It's not his fault if Huey and Toadface thought he'd found the old miser's golden hoard."

I was getting very muzzy and Mulchahe's bulk was getting hard to see. My tongue was getting thick as I mumbled, "It's been up there for fifty years . . . let it stay up there for another fifty. Nobody can ever find it."

"You told me it was there in the old organ chamber."

"Yes, but I didn't tell you how to find it. Besides . . . you wouldn't tell them our secret."

"What makes you think I wouldn't?"

"Cause you're on our side . . . you like us."

"Go to sleep. We'll thrash this out tomorrow. Right now, I have to get back to the theatre and talk to Herlick and Nathan."

I was out before he left the room.

BOOK EIGHT

Anthony Clay Blake

There's a divinity that shapes our ends
Rough-hew them how we will.

Shakespeare, Macbeth, I, 3

CHAPTER TWENTY-FOUR

Marc had invited me out to night lunch. He said he had a great production number he wanted to go over with me. For the last hour or more he had been laying out the scenario.

"Sounds pretty complicated. What's it called?"

"'Tenement Serenade.' It's a terrific number."

"I'm afraid I'll need more time to get all those lyrics right."

His enthusiasm was getting out of control. "Come on. We'll go back by the theater and I'll give you all the lyrics and bits of business."

"The theatre is closed for the night."

"That's all right. I've got a key to the stage door."

When we turned into the alley, the light over the stage door was still lit and there were two burly policemen standing under it.

Marc halted. "Something must've happened."

One of the officers opened the door for us. As we went through the archway to the stage, we both stopped and stared in stunned surprise.

The side drapes were tied back and Mulchahe and O'Brien were standing where they usually hung. Two uniformed officers were mopping a large area near the wings and wringing bloody-looking water into two buckets. Three was a strong smell of ammonia in the air.

Marc glared at the two officers and demanded to know, "What the hell is going on here? What are they doing?"

"They're scrubbing up the blood."

"Blood!" literally howled Marc. "What is blood doing here? Whose blood is it?"

"Huey Ryan's and that little broad, Luttie."

"Huey. . ." Marc gaped at him in stark disbelief. "Huey . . . and. . . Luttie?"

Yeah."

"Well, what happened?" he erupted into a gusher of impotent rage. "Are they all right? Where are they, now?"

"They're in the morgue."

"In the morgue? Then they've been murdered, too." He was badly shaken. "This place is turning into a slaughter house! When will it ever end?"

"It wasn't murder this time." Mulchahe told him. "This time it was an accident."

Marc deflated a bit. "What kind of accident? What happened?"

"We don't have all the answers, yet."

"Couldn't you at least answer a simple question?"

"Yeah. They were up on the catwalk and they fell."

"Why would they be up there after the show was over?" I asked.

"They were going to murder Jade and the kid."

"My God!" gasped Marc. "You're crazy! Why would they want to hurt Jade and Dickie?"

"Jade and the kid had found out why they murdered those other two girls. They couldn't let them live to tell anybody."

"You mean Aidey and Caralyn?"

"Yeah."

"Why would Huey and Hot Crotch want to murder Aidey and Caralyn?" he said, looking at Mulchahe for an answer.

"We don't have all the details, yet."

"Damn dumb assholes," Marc muttered to himself.

The shock had left me speechless. I couldn't believe what they were saying. I couldn't believe Huey had done such a horrible thing. I was afraid to ask about Jade and Dickie.

I finally asked, "Officer, where is Jade and Dickie? Were they . . . were they. . . ?" I couldn't get the words out.

"No. They were roughed up quite a bit, but they're all right. I took them to the hotel and the doctor gave them a powerful jolt of sedatives. They'll be here for the show tomorrow."

"Are you sure Jade's all right?"

"They're both all right."

He got back to being the hard boiled policeman in charge of a gory crime scene. "You guys get out of here and go home." He commanded. Then he barked another order. "And keep your mouths shut. Don't go discussing this with anybody!"

I went back to my room and did some serious thinking. I was almost sure there would be a cover-up. The case would be closed with as little publicity as possible.

I sat there with my mind riding both ends of a seesaw. I knew I had begun to like show business, but I couldn't see myself spending the rest of my life in it. And if it ever became known that I was working in a burlesque theatre when two murders and two bizarre suicides had taken place, I could never live down the stigma. My intelligence tipped the balance.

I packed my bags and called the station for train schedules. Then I obeyed a desire stronger than my will. I knew I couldn't leave without seeing Jade. I had no idea what excuse I'd give for waking her up from a heavily drugged sleep. I wasn't going to tell her I was leaving.

There was no answer when I knocked on her door.

I pounded a little harder. A voice from across the hall yelled, "Knock off the noise out there!"

Then I heard her fumbling with the chain on her door. She opened it a crack and held a puffed, darkening eye to the crack.

"Tony?"

"Yes."

She opened it a bit wider and squinted up at me. She was four inches shorter than usual and she looked as though she'd been sleeping standing on her head. Her hair stood at all angles. Mostly it hung in her eyes.

I put my hand under the tangle to push it back from her face.

"Ouch! My head's sore." She frowned. "Why is my head so sore?" She looked at me with those fabulous green eyes, but she couldn't keep them focused. They wandered somewhere in the area of my face. When she tried to move backward to let me in, her feet got tangled-up with each other.

"What's the matter?" she mumbled. "Did I oversleep? Did you come to get me?"

"No. You've got lots more time to sleep."

"Thank goodness." She weaved back toward the bed. Lifting her knee to crawl in, she saw Dickie's red head on the other side. She regarded it with a long puzzled stare.

"What's Dickie doing here sleeping with me?"

"Looks like he's just sleeping."

"Verry funnnny. You win the putty nose."

Her bewilderment at Dickie being there spilled over in my direction.

"What are you doing here?"

"I came to see if you were all right."

"Course . . . I'm all right . . . why wouldn't I be . . . all right?"

Obviously she wasn't remembering anything about the bloody horror that had happened only a couple of hours ago.

Leaning back against the pillows, she tugged the blanket halfway up over her breast and then gave up the effort. At that moment she had never been more enticing. I'd never wanted her more.

I sat on the edge of the bed, leaned over and kissed her mouth. Her lips were melting, sweet and surrendering. I knew she was half unconscious. I knew I could have her totally. But I forced myself away from her— then cursed myself for being a fool. Why couldn't I just take her and get the gnawing burning desire for her out of my mind and body?

I told myself the taking of her body would leave me on her level. It would mean the loss of my self-respect. But in my heart I knew that once I had possessed her, I'd be chained to the memory for the rest of my life.

Involuntarily my arms went around her and I was lifting her inert body against my chest. I lowered her back down on the pillows. I knew if I started kissing her again the thin layer of my resistance would rupture into rape.

She took a deep shuddering breath. "Please turn-off the lights and fix the door . . . as you leave." Her voice faded out.

I bent and kissed her lips very softly. "Goodby, my darling." Then I remembered the actor's blessing. I raised my hand and said, "Good luck." I turned-off the light and felt my way to the door.

CHAPTER TWENTY-FIVE

Three hours later the streets were still sleeping when I carried my bags out to the waiting taxi.

The waiting room of the station was huge, gloomy and cold; the air was heavy with the odor of unwashed humanity.

People moved around in little whirlpools like lost souls in purgatory hurrying to have their sins expiated.

The train was crowded. There had been a convention in the city, and the home-going revelers filled the seats. All of them in the let-down mood that comes when the clock has struck twelve and the coach and four have turned into a pumpkin and rats.

Yesterday, fired by the stimulus of alcohol and the dementia of belonging, they had been supereminent beings. Tomorrow, dampened by reality, they would slip back into the limbo of mediocrity.

Spasmodically, in a pathetic attempt to stay the regression, a few would burst into raucous off-key harmony that would fade out as the voices trailed off one at a time, like a slowly deflating bagpipe.

As the windows lightened even the desultory snatches of conversation died out—to be replaced by scattered snores that sounded like a chorus of bull alligators. I wondered how the actors could survive so many all night train rides.

I was asleep when the conductor called Lynville.

I let myself into the house and found the hall cold and the door to the library closed. The huge old fireplace in the parlor looked as though no fire had burned in it all winter.

At the farther end of the hall, I found my mother in the den under the back stairs.

"Anthony!" she cried in happy surprise. "Oh, I'm so glad to see you." She stood on tiptoe for my hug.

"I thought I'd better come up and straighten things out for you."

"We can talk about the things tomorrow. . ." She pushed me into one of the deep old chairs. "You sit there and thaw out. You look cold and tired."

After she had filled me in on the home town news, I said, "Shall we start now?"

"There's quite a lot of papers . . . and things," she said.

Going over the papers, and things, I couldn't believe what I was seeing. "Mother, what happened to all the stocks and securities? They can't all be gone—can they?"

"Yes." She spread her hands in a helpless gesture. "It isn't easy to explain."

"Why don't you try." I hoped my annoyance didn't show.

"Well, I knew how important it was for you to make the right impression at the university. And I had to keep up our standard of living. Once people know you're living on the verge of poverty—well, it makes a great deal of difference in your standing in society. I thought I could keep everything going until you and Lela were all settled."

I picked up the notice of foreclosure. "It looks like you failed, mother." Then I saw the tears in her eyes. "It's all right. I'll get it all taken care of."

Later I called Lela and she invited me to dinner that night. When I hung up the phone, my mother came and sat beside me.

"Lela is a mighty fine girl," she said. "Her family is one of the oldest in New England." She hesitated a moment, then said, "And they're one of the richest, too."

"Mother, you're so subtle!"

She looked embarrassed, then said defensively, "Well, we should be realistic."

I walked to the Mellon mansion. Lela met me at the door, looking lovely and self-assured in a pale green dinner gown.

I was vividly conscious of the crystal chandeliers and the priceless furnishings as we walked through the quiet elegance of the drawing room. The Mellon prestige showed.

We sat on a damask couch with a low table in front of it.

"Would you like a drink?"

"Sounds fine."

Minutes later, a maid came in and placed a small tray with the drinks, on the table.

The drinks were relaxing and our talk charming and proper. At first. Then gradually I sensed she was trying to maneuver the chit chat around to something more personal. Each time, I adroitly steered it back to trading chit chat.

Dinner at the Mellon's was a most elegant affair. We had more cocktails in the drawing room, then her mother and father led us through the house to the dining room. The whole place smelled pleasantly of "Essence of Money."

In the glowing light of the candles, in the antique silver candelabrum, the diamonds in Lavinia Mellon's jewelry barely outshone those on Lela. The thought went through my mind that my salary wouldn't buy the shine.

Soon after dinner, her parents left us alone on the divan before the fireplace.

After a long dry spell, she said, "Do you like the place where you work?"

"Yes, but my mother needs me here. I'm considering taking a teaching job here at my father's alma mater."

"Oh, Anthony!" she said in exasperation. "What a stuffy idea. You know Father will give you a position in one of his companies. Something that's important. Something that carries prestige."

"I graduated with a degree in science. I know nothing about the world of high finance."

"That doesn't matter. Father would make all the important decisions. And you'd have an assistant who could make all the minor ones."

And I would be sitting in an office sharpening pencils and making no decisions as all.

It wasn't an appealing prospect.

Men who marry millionaire's daughters and are given a high sounding position in their father's empire are seldom given much respect by their subordinates.

She was quiet for a long spell—probably while the brain selected each plum and laid it neatly in place in her master plan.

"And of course, we'd never have to worry about maintaining a house and a staff of servants. We could always live here."

The Mellon mansion was the grandest in the town, but I'd never dreamed of living in it. It was a heady thought. But . . . something deep in my subconscious told me I didn't want to live in her family's mansion. Neither did I want to be a puppet in one of her father's corporations. It would be a demoralizing way of living. Would they pat me on the head like a newly acquired puppy?

I took her hand in mine—and felt nothing.

I had forced myself away from a woman whose touch could set my whole being on fire, for a woman whose hand felt like every other hand in the world.

I released her hand and reached for my drink.

She regarded her hand as if she were looking for signs of the plague. After a long inspection of her fingernails, she reached for her own drink.

"Did I say something wrong?" she asked with cool politeness.

"There's an old tradition in the Blake family," I said lightly. "When a son marries, he always brings his bride back to the ancestral home. I had planned on keeping that old tradition alive."

In the lull that followed, you could almost hear the rusty hinges of tradition creaking.

Finally she said, "But your home is ever so much too small." She waved her hand to take in her domain. Our home has two large suites that aren't being used. The east wing is very large, it would be absolutely perfect for us. It's completely private."

I searched my mind for a noncommittal answer. An answer that didn't usher me into the east wing but still left the door open. No suitable answer presented itself. I kissed her fingertips and said nothing.

"Did you get your mother's little problem taken care of?" she asked with forced interest.

"There really wasn't anything to worry about." I was becoming very adept at lying.

Suddenly I was bored with all the hedging, the dodging and sidestepping the quicksand.

I stood up, pulled her to her feet and put my arms around her. "Actually, there is still a couple of details I have to see about. Tomorrow I'll take care of them, and see you tomorrow night."

She brightened and said, "Bring your mother to dinner tomorrow night. We'll have a family conclave. I'm sure daddy can find a solution to any problem she has."

Kissing her goodnight was pleasant, but it started no tomtoms beating in my chest.

That night I sat in the den long after my mother had gone upstairs to bed.

The flames dancing among the logs in the fireplace made shadows like dancers leaping and weaving on the stage. Gradually, the dancers melted into the embers and there was only one wraith dancing against the blackened background. The green fire that flickered off the tips of the flames was like the green fire that sometimes crackled behind her eyes.

I began picturing Jade living here in this staid old house, then smiled at the absurd illusion. Most of her waking hours, she lived in a world of make-believe.

Once I asked her if she liked living in that cheap two-penny world.

"Yes! I love it! You can dance on the arc of a rainbow, or you can sob your heart out in hell—but at least, you know you're alive." She made a gesture of pure ecstacy. "And the sweetest music this side of the Hallelujah Hosanna is that burst of applause that makes the rafters ring."

"To an actor, perhaps. To other people it would probably be just a lot of raucous noise."

"Oh indubitably," she said with a haughty ultra-affected smirk. "Everything depends on one's audiovisual perspective. To the Americans, Paul Revere was a clarion-voiced patriot. To the British, he was just a big blabber-mouth."

She gave me a pitying smile. "Anything beats sitting at a desk all day long making marks on a piece of paper. What a deadly way to spend your life."

At the time, I had assured her it was the only way I wanted to spend mine. Now, frankly, it didn't seem so great.

The dancing flames had a hypnotic effect. A log burned in two in the middle and the flames leaped up like colored lights leaping to life on a darkened stage.

I was wholly unaware of the comparisons as they began to creep into my reveries, like the easy camaraderie of life backstage compared to the stiff formality of life in the Mellon mansion.

Jade with her sharp sense of humor and her throaty laugh compared to Lela, who thought any show of comic humor would crack her social decorum and laughter above one decibel was low and gauche.

Then there were those ritualistic Sunday night suppers at the Mellon mansion, with always the correct number of guests, being served faultlessly by mute servants. Once I thought those suppers were the highest plateau in gracious living. Now I realized they had all the gaiety of a funeral mass. A ham'ugger sam'itch was more appealing.

I had a vision of those Sunday night suppers stretching down through the years to the end of my life. It would be a bleak and boring journey.

There had always been a tacit understanding between both our families that Lela and I would marry. But we had never become formally engaged because I had never asked her to marry me.

There was a growing sense of relief as I slowly began to realize I was not obligated to honor their expectations of me. That realization gave me a glowing sense of freedom. With a surge of elation, I knew I would never spend any part of my life in the east wing of the old Mellon mansion!

Next morning when I entered the den, my mother was reading the society section. She lowered the paper and said, "Did you have a nice evening with Lela?" The question was overloaded with hopeful expectations.

"Yes, it was very pleasant."

"Lela called and asked us to dinner, tonight."

"Sorry, Mother, we'll have to cancel. We're going to have a very tiring day. First we have to straighten out the mortgage business. When we're through with that, I'll have to start making plans for finding a job—if we want to continue eating."

She made some optimistic remarks about how everything would work out all right. She finished by saying, "Of course it may be quite a strain at first."

That was a monumental understatement, but I let it pass.

We spent most of the day haggling with Mister Hammond

at the bank. After a lot of time thrashing out the details, he agreed not to foreclose if I met each note as it came due, plus paying one that was past due. Then there were new papers to be drawn up and signed. When everything was settled, I was mentally exhausted.

That night, I considered, and rejected, a few different jobs. There really weren't too many choices.

I had definitely decided I didn't want to be a teacher. And Lynville didn't have too many other golden opportunities to offer a junior-grade scientist.

Next day was Friday, a bad day to go job hunting, so I took my mother to lunch and a matinee. Besides, I needed the weekend to do some thinking about my future.

The weekend came and went and my future was still as vague as ever. I had left resumes at several firms. Now there was nothing to do but wait for results.

During the mornings, I made the rounds to see if any of my resumes had found fertile soil. Then spent the rest of the day playing recordings of the popular singers or sitting at the piano practicing different singing styles and phrasings.

Time crawled along like an arthritic caterpillar.

At night, after my mother had gone upstairs to bed, I sat in the den and watched the flames recreating scenes from behind a door I had closed forever. I watched the darkened stage come to life, an Egyptian harem with beautiful slave girls dancing for the king. Above the sound of the music, I could hear the swishing whisper of their sandals against the polished floor. But the scenes that followed me upstairs and kept me from sleeping, were those of Jade dancing in the colored spotlight while I stood behind the proscenium and sang to her.

In spite of the assurance to myself that I wanted no part of show business, especially the tawdry world of burlesque, my mind was constantly filled with the memory of it. My thoughts kept asking questions. Why had I left in the middle of a show? Was it because I had to get away because I was afraid to stay until the end of the week? Afraid I might weaken and stay on?

Other questions kept creeping in. Would they hire me back? Who would have the say? I knew Marc would be on my side, despite his screaming tirades about that stupid amateur who didn't know his ass from a hole-in-the-ground!

Tracy would be for me. Thoughts of Tracy brought a smile. Tracy, with her barbed wit, hiding an innate kindness.

Darlene. who assured me, "The first hundred years are the hardest—after that it doesn't get hard!" She would definitely be on my team.

BOOK NINE

Jade LeMare

You're blown like a leaf on the winds of time
With a million leaves of your kind
Your destiny is borne of the mindless wind
You soar—You fly—You wither—You die
The winds of time blow swiftly on
Oblivious of dead leaves left behind

Irish

CHAPTER TWENTY-SIX

It was a very unpleasant dream, someone was gouging my eye out. When I awoke, there was a wash cloth on my temple dripping cold water into my ear and down my neck. Two stubby thumbs were forcing my eye as wide open as the Grand Canyon.

Dickie was staring anxiously into the pit. "Jade . . . Jade . . . why don't you wake up? Your eyes look funny."

They'll look blind when you get through with them!"

"Do you know your face is all swolled up an' nat eye is all blue lookin' an ya got a lump right beside it?"

He pointed out the lump by poking it with his finger.

"Ouch . . . you. . ."

I held the wash cloth against the sore lump while the details of yesterday's horror slowly came together in my still drug-fuzzy thoughts.

The scene in the organ chamber. That malevolent toad swinging the pry bar at Dickie's head. Huey. Charming Huey with his infectious smile. What had tipped the balance to Huey the cruel murderer with the trickline in his hand?

I knew I would always feel a deep sadness when I remembered Huey.

And that awful scene on the stage below the catwalk. Could I ever forget those screams of mortal terror as I watched Luttie frantically clutching for a handhold in empty air. It was a shock to realize I didn't care. I knew I'd never feel any pity for Old Hot Crotch.

Dickie was still groggy. He yawned widely and I thought he was going back to sleep. He yawned and said sleepily, "Jade, I had th' terriblest awfulest dream . . . We wuz up there on th' catwalk an' nen we wuz down on th'stage. . ."

"That was some dream."

He brushed the hair out of his eyes and his hand hit the crusted knot on his forehead. He flinched and looked puzzled.

"Jade, did they hit us?"

"No. You bumped your head on my sink." There was no way I could bring my self to rehash the grisly horror for him. I'd let Tramp and Arlete do the explaining. Mercifully, the drug had blotted out some of it. Hopefully in time, it would fade into a hazy memory.

"Come on, get dressed. We'll stop and have your favorite breakfast, pancakes and syrup."

"Did Tramp and Arlete say I could stay all night with you?"

"They must have, you're here, aren't you?"

He examined me critically. "Why's your eye all swolled up?"

"I bought some new eye make-up. I must be real allergic to it."

"It's sure gonna take a lot of make-up to fix your face this morning."

"I'll put a lot of black around my eyes and pretend I'm a witch."

"Whatta mean, pretend?"

"Unfunny comic."

Tramp and Arlete were waiting in the lobby. They practically smothered Dickie with hugs and kisses.

I gave them a high-five and pantomimed not to talk about last night.

Dickie had his story book under his arm. He handed it to Tramp and said, "Me and Jade didn't read any stories las' night."

He yawned widely, "We jus' went to sleep." He frowned, "An' I got a bump on my head, somehow . . . an' I want some pancakes and syrup."

We were lucky enough to get to the theatre before the others started arriving.

Tracy came in while I was blending greasepaint over the dark bruise on my forehead. "How do you feel?" she asked. "Do you think you can do the show?"

"Yes, I'm all right . . . I guess. You know . . . the show must go on."

"So they say."

"Jade, what really happened? Nobody is saying anything at all."

"I don't want to talk about it. It was so gruesome . . . so horrible. Besides I have strict orders not to talk about it to anyone."

"I'm surprised you're even here."

"I wonder why there are no scareheads in the papers this morning," I said.

"The powers that be have a lot of clout. I'm sure they've put a muzzle on everybody in the theatre," she said. "Although there isn't anything they could tell, since nobody knows what did happen. . ."

"Mulchahe and O'Brien were there. They know exactly what happened . . . and why."

"Herlick and Nathan had a meeting with them up in the office this morning. Mulchahe must've agreed to go along with whatever they said."

"They said the case is closed. They're calling it an accident."

"That's ridiculous!"

"It's one way out of the mess. I guess they figured they couldn't convict two dead bodies for murder."

Marc knocked and came in. He looked utterly dejected.

Tracy took his hand. "Don't let it get you, Marc. Everybody is shocked out of their senses. It's a nightmare. But, at least it's all over. Nothing else could possibly happen."

"Yes it can. Tony jumped the show last night."

"What! Are you sure? How do you know?"

"I gave him some lyrics last night. I just now called to remind him to bring them in with him. The hotel clerk said he had checked out last night."

"It never rains," she moaned. "We just have cloudbursts!"

Marc left and I sat there feeling like the bottom had dropped out of the world. I couldn't hold back the tears. "Crying won't help", said Tracy.

"He didn't even say goodbye," I sobbed.

"Don't cry anymore," she blotted my tears. "You look bad enough already."

She went out and I cried a great deal more.

The matinee was a mish-mash. Tracy was steering Barry through Tony's scenes and throwing him lyrics from behind the curtain.

When I went out for my number, I asked Tracy, "How's it going?"

"About like Dockstodder's Minstrels doing a wake."

Herlick and Nathan were encamped in Huey's office. They had stationed an uniformed officer at the stage door with orders to let no one in except the actors. Any reporter that came around was to be sent to their office. I suppose enough green salve will cure the most persistent case of curiosity.

During the next couple of days, things started settling back into something like the normal routine. I spent a lot of time putting ice on my swollen eyes.

I had finished hiding the most visible signs of my puffy eyes when there was an imperious knock on my door.

"Come in," I called.

A tall elegantly dressed man with a high forehead and a higher opinion of himself walked in. He introduced himself as Robert Callaway—attorney for the Herlick and Nathan enterprise.

"How do you do?" I held out my hand.

He looked me over with a grimace that people usually reserve for cockroaches, pulpy worms and other creepy crawly creatures.

"Won't you sit down?"

He began removing his hat and overcoat and I would have bet all the marbles he'd rehearsed the stylized routine before a mirror. He seated himself just-so and crossed one alligator-shod foot across the opposite knee.

He fished out a note book and cleared his throat.

His pedantic legalese was calculated to bamboozle me in nothing flat.

When he ran down, I gave him a vacant-eyed stare with my mouth hanging open, picked my nose and inspected my fingernail.

"I don't know what'cer talkin' about," I said stupidly.

"I'd advise you to think about the legal trouble you could find yourself in," he intoned. "I'll see you tomorrow, when you've had more time to think it over." His tone implied I was totally incapable of thinking anything over.

As he was going through his routine of getting back into his coat and hat, Mulchahe's imposing bulk filled the open doorway.

"Mister Callaway, this is Lieutenant Mulchahe," I said.

Mister Callaway shed his arrogance and other nasties like a snake shedding its skin. "I'm an attorney for Herlick and Nathan." he shook hands with another rehearsed gesture.

"Better count your fingers, Lieutenant."

Mister Callaway's head jerked around as though a bee had invaded his ear. His fish-belly complexion turned a dull red.

"You haven't seen the last of me", he said.

"Oh dear, I was hoping I had."

"What was that all about?" asked Mulcahe.

"Oh, that five-star phony!"

"What did he want?"

"He wanted to scare me to death."

"With what?"

"He came in here with his cannons loaded, and started threatening me with all kinds of dire things that could happen to me if I tried to get smart. He told me that anything found in this old theatre would be the property of the owners. He said . . . Hey wait a minute . . . how would they know I'd found anything in this theatre? Did you tell them?"

"No, no I didn't. As soon as I got back to the theatre last night, after I took you and the kid home, they were waiting for me. They were anxious to find out what happened. I told them we saw Huey and the little broad take the kid up the ladder, and heard them make him call you. I said we climbed up the ladder in time to hear Huey tell you he had murdered those two girls because they each had a twenty dollar gold piece. I told them he thought you and the kid had found a lot of the gold pieces and he was trying to make you tell him where they were. I said when Huey saw us, he knew they were trapped, so he flipped the little broad over the rail and then he jumped."

"You sorta rewrote the script, didn't you?"

"Basically no. That was what happened, wasn't it?"

"That and a few other things. What did they say when you told them about Huey and Luttie?"

"They kept making comments about how strange it was that Huey could do such a terrible thing. I asked permission to search Huey's desk. I found the two gold pieces Huey had taken from those two girls. They were in a locked drawer."

"They couldn't have known where the coins came from originally."

"I'd say it took them about half a minute to guess. They couldn't have owned this theatre all these years without hearing something about the old miser who built the place and the rumors about him hiding a fortune in gold somewhere in it."

"So, let them guess. They can't guess where it is."

"I'd say it took them another minute to figure out that Huey and the little broad didn't force you and the kid to go up on that catwalk to have a picnic."

He looked down at me. "How long do you think it took them to figure out that Huey and the little broad didn't force you and the kid to go up on that catwalk to have a picnic."

He looked down at me. "How long do you think it took them to figure out you and the kid must know something about the gold. Why do you think they sent their attorney to see you?"

"Are you sure you didn't tell them about all those cigar boxes up there—filled with twenty dollar gold pieces?"

"I didn't see any boxes filled with gold pieces."

"That's right," I crowed. "You didn't see them, so you don't know where they are. And if they searched for a million years, they couldn't find them! Only Dickie and I know the Open Sesame. They'll never know if Dickie found two gold coins, or if we unearthed the Crown Jewels of Ireland."

"Maybe you'd better tell them."

"No. Then they'd have all the snipes, and Dickie and I would be left holding the bag."

His look said I was a pea-brained idiot, but he would try to bear up.

I picked up the puff and patted powder over my face, trying to erase the haggard look. I sighed and said, "Did yesterday really happen? Or was the whole thing just a horror movie?"

"It would be better if you didn't think about it."

"Do you think they'll buy your version?"

"They'll have to," he said. "This way, they can only publish what we tell them."

"Yes, of course. What they don't know can't hurt us."

"We think we've covered all the loose ends."

I gazed at that imposing bulk and knew I was going to miss Mulchahe. What had been my granite enemy was now my granite friend.

"Lieutenant Mulchahe. . ."

He cocked a quizzical eyebrow.

"Will you be coming backstage anymore?"

"Probably not. The case is closed."

"Your case is closed. Mine isn't."

"You really are not going to give up, are you?"

"No, I'm not."

"You know you could be in a lot of danger. They might decide to play by Huey's rules."

I stared at him in dismay. "I never thought about that. Maybe it was because I felt safe with you around. "Now I will be afraid." I said. "I need you to tell me what to do."

He reflected on that. "In that case, maybe I'd better keep coming around for awhile."

CHAPTER
TWENTY-SEVEN

Those next few days were the longest I've ever lived through. I had opened a Pandora's box for myself, and couldn't close it.

During the day, I tried to fend off Old Fish-belly's dire threats and questions. During the nights, I cried myself to sleep over that blue-blooded, black-hearted snob.

This morning Tracy was getting a cup of tea when I came into the green room. She handed me a cup and said "Why don't you just give up?"

"Give up what?"

"Running to the mail box every morning to see if perchance Tony might've sent you a card."

"Silly, isn't it? He doesn't know I'm living. He was nuts about you. But there was no way he'd ever allow himself to become involved with a woman in show business—especially in burlesque."

"Yeah, I know. Actors and their ilk never have been re-garded as being respectable."

"That's right. Therefore you could never be in his class. "He's got all those generations of breeding behind him."

"So has a jersey bull, but I wouldn't fall in love with one."

"Bravo Punchinello!" she began singing. "Even though your heart is breaking, laugh clown laugh!"

"Go do your Pagliacchi act somewhere else, will you?"

"You'll get over it," she handed me the tube of greasepaint. "In the meantime—Vesti La Guibba. The show must go on."

Vest La Guibba! I began smearing on the greasepaint.

On intermission, Mulchahe loomed in my doorway.

"Where've you been?" I demanded.

"We got tied up with a case," he sat down in the old chair groaning in protest. "How are things coming along?"

"Like a toe-dancer with the gout."

"That bad?"

"Worse."

He made a comment about people who couldn't swim stay-ing out of deep water.

"You're right. I'm in way over my head."

"What are you going to do?" he asked seriously.

"I honestly don't know. It's like a merry-go-round that won't stop and let me off."

"Has Mister Callaway been back?"

"OH YES."

"Did you get anything settled?"

"I told him I'd show where a million or two in gold was. If he'd make them sign an ironbound agreement to put a hundred thousand dollars in a trust fund for Dickie."

He raised his eyebrow in amused surprise. "I thought it was going to be fifty thousand."

"I upped the ante."

"What did he say?"

"He said I was crazy."

"I'm beginning to believe him."

"Crazy or not, I'm still the player with all the aces up her sleeve."

"You're playing against some smart players. They know how to stack the deck. I'd suggest you throw in your cards."

"Not on your life! Old Fish-belly is just shoveling smoke. They'll do anything to get their hands on a million dollars."

"Do you know how much money is actually up there?"

"There is about fifty or sixty big old cigar boxes in that little room. I lifted the lids off a lot of them. They were all full. Then I counted the gold pieces in three of them. Each one had six thousand dollars in it."

He whistled.

"Those twenty dollar gold pieces are worth a lot more today than they were when that old miser stashed them up there."

"That sounds like a lot of money." he observed.

I never could tell, by looking at his face, whether he believed what I was saying.

"Lieutenant Mulchahe . . ." I began lamely. "You were right. I'm way out of my league. I've got the winning hand, but I don't know how to play it . . . if I tell them where the money is they'll find some way to out-smart me. . ."

"You can bet on it," he said.

"So . . . would you . . . please be my negotiator? Please . . . you'd know how to deal with them. They'd know they couldn't put anything over on you."

"What makes you think I could out negotiate Satan for Hades. But . . . I'll have to think about it."

"What's there to think about. All you have to do is tell them if they don't sign the agreement, they will never see any of that money. Tell them anything. Tell them I'm nutty enough to burn the theatre down to keep them from ever finding all that nice shiny gold money!"

When he sorta nodded I felt a rush of excitement. Had I persuaded him to play the role of my conspirator?

He gave me an arch smile. "Yeah, I think they might be inclined to negotiate the deal with me. In fact, I'll bet they would do just about anything to get rid of you."

"And get their hands on all that money!" I thought I'd better stress some of the important points. "When you take them up there, be sure to watch the hands that are lifting the lids on those boxes!"

"Oh? Do I have to take them up there?" He sounded like he didn't relish another trip up that ladder.

"Certainly! If you let them go up there alone, they'd steal the money and swear the boxes were empty."

I took Dickie's magnet from under the pillow on the daybed and handed it to him. I explained the approximate location of the panel and told him how to get it open. I thought he still looked a bit dubious.

Be sure to make them play according to the Mulchahe of Queensbury rules," I said.

He shook his head, "Things are going to be mighty dull around this place when you leave."

"Ha, they're lucky I'm not demanding a reward for myself as well as Dickie."

"Don't get too cocky," he said. "They might get mean."

"In other words, don't insult the alligator until after you've crossed the river."

He actually laughed.

CHAPTER
TWENTY-EIGHT

With Mulchahe leading the charge, we had won the war. The battle was over. The armistice had been signed. The spoils had been divided.

Dickie had a college fund, the Gruesome Twosome had an extra million or two. And me? I could now go back to my crossword puzzles, sewing on sequins and doing my needlepoint.

Then why wasn't I going into my bells?

Because the end of the charade had been a sharp letdown.

Actors love to act. When they're on stage they forget about everything else. No matter what the role, we always pad our part. We stay on stage as long as we can. We can make a production out of a walk-across.

Playing Sherlock for Mulchahe and crossing swords with old Fish-belly, not only allowed me to be a Walter Mitty, it had kept my love-sick yearnings at bay. Now that the excitement was over, they came crowding back with a force that left me teary-eyed and miserably unhappy.

Each day I vowed I would never fall in love again.

Each night I wondered if I would ever fall out of love.

Today was another opening day, and the little blue devils were already sharpening their pitchforks.

Marc was out in the hall pitching a hissy. Whatever the problem was, heaven wasn't coming through with a solution.

I was applying my siren mask, when Dickie came in with a book under his arm. He climbed into the old chair and sat there waiting for me to say something.

"Get out of here, Dickie."

"I knowed you wuz goin' to be mean. I could tell by lookin' at you. Why're you so mean?"

"This is opening day."

"Every week has a openin' day."

"All right. What do you want?"

"Don't you think I've been learnin' to read, purty good?"

"I'd give you a 'B,'" I said. "Why?"

"Well . . . Arlete got me this new story book, but it looks like it's for bigger kids. So, if I can't read some of the words. I'll spell them and you can tell me what they mean, okay?"

"Okay."

He struggled through the first few pages of one story, but his chagrin kept rising with every sentence.

"Jeez Chris!" he finally exploded. "This book is dumb. Who'd wanna read this stuff?" A princess . . . who could feel a pea through twelve mattresses just wasn't in the realm of his believability.

He looked toward the door, curled his lip in heavy disgust and said, "We wuz just sittin' here mindin' our own business, when in flew a dead duck!"

I turned and looked toward the door—and all the morning glory bells started ringing and all the little blue devils ran and hid.

Mister Anthony Clay Blake was standing in my doorway!

Dickie managed to stomp on his foot as he charged out the door.

"Jade . . ."

I knew what he was going to say—but I didn't want him to say it. I was hopelessly in love with him, but I had never even dreamed of marrying him. It's a wise woman who knows her limitations. Therefore I needed no Einstein brain to tell me that marrying Tony Blake would be the worst misalliance in history.

Even besotted by love, I knew I did not have the social finesse to play the role of wife to a Brahmin like Tony Blake. I hadn't been born with that little black book of rules clutched in my hand.

He came on into the room, took my hand and said, "Jade . . . will you marry me?"

"I hesitated all of three seconds before I said, "Yes."

After all, why tell a man you're not good enough for him? Let him find it out for himself.

FINALE

About the Author

Janne Cafara, by some predestined path, found her way into the enchanted world of make-believe called show business. Theaters were her school and actors her teachers. She learned to dance, read lines, how to laugh and how to cry, on cue. Her coaches taught her high drama and low comedy, and everything else came by osmosis, even feeling the heart beat of the audience.

Janne played such roles as: Little Eva, demure ingenues, frivolous soubrettes and silky sirens. She danced in the chorus of Tabloid shows, musical reviews and Broadway productions. The theater was her castle and the stage door, her magic portal through which she traveled from beggar to queen. Inside the castle Janne learned the priceless lesson of perfect timing and gained her greatest reward—the art of doing comedy. Burlesque was her game—Empress was her fame.

Janne Cafara starred in productions across the United States during the 1940's, 50's and 60's. Ms. Cafara resides in San Diego.